DRACULA TRANSFORMED
& Other Bloodthirsty Tales

DRACULA
TRANSFORMED
& Other Bloodthirsty Tales

Mark McLaughlin & Michael McCarty

WILDSIDE PRESS

CONTENTS

A special dedication: Michael McCarty and Mark McLaughlin wish to thank three fine individuals who have inspired both of us: Bram Stoker, Mel Piff, and Joyce Godwin Grubbs.

Mark would like to thank: Michael S. Jr. for his unwavering support and kindness. Also, I'd like to thank my good friends Michael and Cindy McC., John B. and the gang at Wildside Press, The Amazing Kreskin, and C. Dean Andersson. I'd also like to thank all the B-movie monsters lurking on my movie shelves … Dracula, the Tingler, Frankenstein's Monster, the Creature from the Black Lagoon, the Mummy, King Kong, Gamera and his many monstrous foes, Godzilla, Space-Godzilla, MechaGodzilla, Hedorah, Gigan, King Ghidorah, Mothra, Space Amoeba, the Black Scorpion, the Wasp Woman, and every sort of zombie imaginable. Love ya!

Michael would like to thank: Cindy McCarty and Latte, John Betancourt and Wildside Press, the memory of Kitty, Bev and Daisy Mae, Steve McCarty and family, Jody, Linnea Quigley, Larry Nadolsky, Bonnie Lou, Lyle Ernst, Katy, Holly, Joe McKinney, Renée Bushā, Elvira, Chef Steph, Brian Kronfeld, Christopher Lee, Bela Lugosi, Jean Brandt, Christopher and Valerie Miron, the Hultings, the Leonards, The Amazing Kreskin, C. Dean Andersson, The Source Bookstore, Joe Mynhardt, Connie Sherwood, The Book Rack, Brad Cook, The Thompsons and of course, my friend and collaborator, Mark.

Published by Wildside Press LLC.
www.wildsidepress.com

INTRODUCTION

by The Amazing Kreskin

Yours truly has been a tremendous fan of great Gothic horror stories. For my own taste, I would pick of the classics, the greatest … *Dracula*. Oh yes, we have *Frankenstein*, which Shelley managed to put together on that rainy vacation period in England, and resulted in a dramatic creation of a monster. Bram Stoker went far beyond such in creating the character of Dracula, who has such a large dynamic dimension in the story that this mysterious being of evil has continued to entrance audiences for over a century.

It is with great excitement that I introduce you to a new presentation by Mark McLaughlin and Mike McCarty entitled: *Dracula Transformed*. I am quite familiar with Michael McCarty's talent, what with his major contribution to my book, *Conversations with Kreskin*. Let me go beyond that, as his prolific writings in the past have so often lead us into the area of Gothic horror. Mark McLaughlin could not have found a better partner in teaming up with Michael McCarty. Please don't misunderstand me: I can assure you McCarty is not a vampire, although I'm not so certain that he wouldn't feel at home embracing the character.

Now let me prepare you for McCarty and McLaughlin's new contribution. If you've read Stoker's *Dracula* in the past, or seen the classic movies of *Dracula*, prepare yourself to be fascinated with this presentation—one you're going to find increasingly delectable. What is neat is they have found out how Dracula survived in spite of the early attacks from the Vampire expert, Dr. Van Helsing. Boy, it is remarkable how they've expanded on what makes Dracula the most fascinating character of all the Gothic monsters. Far more than just someone who's had a brain put inside his head in a laboratory.

Dracula continues to possess the extraordinary power of hypnotizing others by mere glances, as well as using his telepathic ability. All this and the extension of life even after death, is mesmerizing.

They've done it so legitimately that yours truly was taken aback on how Renfield has returned to the scene of Dracula's existence, and if you think the three wives have disappeared after all these many years, boy, will you be in for a surprise, just as much as you will when a character enters the scene from the Gothic past who will turn out to be invisible! You'll even be reminded of a man who I saw on the stage and in movies, playing Dracula, Bela Lugosi. Oh yes, how in the world Dracula would ever enter the Las Vegas scene of today … well, prepare yourself for a shock. You will not forget the scenarios that take place in the gambling capitol of the world. What a diabolical touch that Dracula enters the United States. You heard me, not just England, but the United States, including parts of New Jersey. I will not be driving through certain towns or areas here in NJ without recalling the visit of the King of the Vampires to this State.

I predict that you're going to be hypnotized by the pages to follow. You'll find them invigorating, and at times chilling. I wonder if you will also agree with me that this could be a damn refreshing motion picture. As these pages unfold, you can't help wondering who today should play Dracula. Don't worry about it—for the time being, prepare yourself for these pages filled with electricity.

LUCY TRANSFORMED

by Michael McCarty & Mark McLaughlin

Editor's Note: The following letters were found in an otherwise empty coffin, in a tomb in a Parisian cemetery. Above the door of the tomb, the name ZALESKA is carved in marble. No surname or dates of birth or death can be found anywhere on the structure. Only a few facts are known about the missing occupant: it is said that she was very pale, enjoyed late-night parties, and would often joke that her father was the most famous of all vampires.

* * * *

My little one,

How I relished your last letter! It cheers me to no end to learn that you are enjoying Paris. Of course, you are so very beautiful, like your departed mother, Ilona—I am sure that before long, the entire city will be in love with you. Drain them dry, Zaleska, my thirsty angel.

You will be delighted to know that I have decided to follow your example. I am making plans to leave our homeland and establish a new home in England, and when all is prepared, perhaps you can come and stay with me. It has been so long since I last talked with you. As much as I enjoy your letters, it is not the same as hearing your lovely low voice. It is like the purr of a tiger, your voice.

It is good for us to venture forth into the world. Our family has ruled our homeland for centuries. We have survived wars, famines, diseases, even foolish attempts at assassination. We have spilled so much blood onto the soil, it would bleed if you stabbed into it with a sword. But it is just small corner of the world—your letters have made me realize this, my darling daughter! I need to see new places. I need to drink deep from new throats. I wonder if the blood of the English will have a different flavor? I shall soon know. They are pampered, these English folks. I am sure their blood will be sweet and creamy, like that of a fat calf.

After extensive correspondence with real estate firms across England, I am purchasing a great many fine properties. My latest acquisition is a place called Carfax Abbey, located near the community of Whitby, England. The firm I have selected to assist me with this transaction assigned to me a representative named Peter Hawkins, who came with the highest of recommendations.

Mr. Hawkins and I corresponded for several weeks and he agreed to come to Transylvania to finalize the legal details of the purchase. I informed him that when he arrived at the Borgo Pass, I would have a carriage ready for him.

Of course, I have no driver. Like so many maids and housekeepers over the years, he ended up being my dinner during lean times. But that was not a problem. I drove the coach myself, disguised in a hat and thick black coat. I found the idea amusing. Now you can see why I need to travel! I am so desperate for new sensations, I enjoyed the very thought of such a foolish ruse.

After the other coach dropped off my guest, he boarded my carriage and we headed to the castle. It was a night of wild winds and dazzling moonlight. The wolves began to howl in the moonlight, a choir of night creatures singing their hungry song. You used to run with the wolves when you were a little girl, all black hair, white skin and dark flashing eyes. Do you still remember your playmates, the wolves?

I stopped the horses in the courtyard, then leaped down to assist my passenger. I helped him out of the carriage, but my grip must have been too strong for him. He winced and gritted his little square teeth! You would have thought I had put his hand in a vise.

After I showed him into the castle, I went to my own quarters and changed into my evening clothes. I then returned to my guest. It turns out my visitor was not Mr. Hawkins at all, but a younger member of the firm named Jonathan Harker. Apparently Mr. Hawkins was too sick with gout to make the trip. Gout! An illness for self-indulgent old simpletons. How disappointing, to learn that my supposed champion was the sort who suffered from such a disease. It was like hearing that a mother superior suffers from the French pox.

Mr. Harker explained that in his occupation, he was often called upon to explain the intricacies of purchasing British property to foreign buyers. He also informed me that he had succeeded in his examinations and was now a full-blown solicitor. His people love their titles and rules. I have never been one to worry about rules. What will they think of me, I wonder!

I made sure he enjoyed a good dinner. I let him know I had dined already, and indeed, that was true. I'd satisfied my needs with a fat farmer on a rural road earlier that evening.

I gave Mr. Harker some roast chicken, cheese, a salad and a bottle of wine. During his meal, he talked about the museums of England and his finance, Miss Mina Murray. They are to be wed when he returns home. He showed me her image, set in a locket. She is quite lovely—as lovely as you and your mother. I will need to meet this Miss Mina while I am in England.

After dinner, we sat in the study by the fireplace. Mr. Harker smoked a cigar. In your last letter, you mentioned that so many people in Paris enjoy smoking. Such a filthy habit. Though I imagine that those who smoke may not look too kindly on our appetites. But still, to breathe in the poisons from a fire—how absurd! Some people do insist on rushing to their graves.

In time, I bid Mr. Harker good night. I let him know that I would be absent during the day but would talk with him more when night returned again. Later that night, I set out his breakfast, along with a pot of coffee.

I soon realized that I would have problems with folks in England who insisted on conducting business during the day. I've decided that I will need to find a weak-minded, weak-willed servant to help me. Someone who is easily controlled and will do what I ask of him. It will have to be a man, but not one like your uncle Radu, who enjoys the caress of other men. It cannot be someone who might fall in love with me. A servant who loves me might decide to end my existence and then commit suicide, so we can be together in death. I am telling you this so that you, too, will observe those precautions should you decide to take on a servant. Make sure it is a servant who worships you, but would not be inclined to lust for you.

The next evening, I opened the door to my library and found Mr. Harker looking through my books. I was quite amused to watch as he picked up the *Necronomicon,* a very rare book for which I had to kill to obtain my copy. He does not know Latin, so the text meant nothing to him, but I could see that he found the illustrations most disturbing.

He quickly put down the book and piled others on top of it, to hide it from his sight!

It was through books that I decided to explore the possibility of England as a new home. The authors of that land write such poetic, meaningful tales. And the tales of London! It must be wondrous— a city where the streets are filled with activity, and plenty of fresh blood, too! I am eager to walk through those crowded streets—to be in the midst of that mad rush. I imagine you feel the same when you walk through Paris.

Here in my homeland, I belong to the highest rank of Romanian aristocracy. The common people recognize me as their master and would never dream of rising up against me. But in England, I might be looked upon as a strange—and strangers are often regarded with suspicion.

With these thoughts in mind, I asked Mr. Harker if he could stay with me for a few weeks, so that we could talk more. Such conversations would help me to improve my enunciation of English words. When I arrive in England, I do not want to have a thick accent that would be considered foreign. I also asked if he could help me to cultivate an appearance that would blend in with the populace.

"I will certainly do my best to help you," he said. He is so accommodating. But then, he wants the sale to proceed smoothly, so it is in his best interest for him to please me.

I let him know that he could go anywhere he wish within the castle, if the doors he encountered were unlocked. Locked rooms are sealed for a reason. As I said to him, "We are in Transylvania, and Transylvania is not England."

He responded to that with a polite laugh! He would not laugh if he knew what was behind those doors. I have other guests in the castle besides him.

Also, some of your experiments still live in those rooms, my child, even though they are rarely fed. I have always admired your scientific mind. Perhaps someday you will return to your studies, when you tire of flirting with Frenchmen.

Do give some thought to visiting me in England. It will wonderful to see you again, after so many years!

With love,
Father

* * * *

My little one,

I am quite excited by the prospect of residing in England. This evening, Mr. Harker told me much about Carfax Abbey, which goes back to medieval times. The house, he said, has high stone walls and magnificent iron gates. The place is next to an old chapel, with many dense groupings of trees on the land, as well as a deep lake. There are a few other houses in the area of Carfax Abbey, one being a large building which hosts a private lunatic asylum. Mr. Harker assured me that the asylum is not visible from the grounds, and certainly that is just as well. I would tire of mad eyes constantly staring in my direction.

Our conversation carried on for hours. Then I heard the rooster crow and realized, it was time for my rest.

I returned to talk with Mr. Harker when a new stretch of night arrived. This time, I found him shaving by the window in his room. He had hung a small mirror on the wall for that purpose.

I greeted him and my voice must have startled him, for he cut himself by accident. Instantly, the sweet smell of his blood filled the room.

Mr. Harker looked at me, then the mirror, then back to me again. He may have noticed that I do not cast a reflection. I looked at the blood as it trickled slowly down the side of his neck. The sight of that fresh blood threw me into a ravenous fury. I grabbed at his throat. He sought to steady himself, and by chance, grabbed the string of beads and crucifix he had placed on a nearby side table.

The sight of that vile crucifix caused me to regain my composure. Somehow, I found the words needed to explain away my impetuous behavior.

"This wretched thing has done the mischief. Away with it!" I seized the shaving mirror and flung it out the window. The glass shattered on the stones of the courtyard below. "I cannot stand mirrors. Such frivolous toys! They excite one's vanity, and no man needs that."

After I left the room, I lock all the main doors, making Mr. Harker a prisoner in my castle. I did not want him wandering away or talking with any of the local people.

The next evening, I met with him again. I have three lovely

guests staying with me in the castle. Lovely, but not as lovely as you or your mother, I assure you. But they do share your ravenous thirst! Up until that point, they had all been content to stay locked in their various chambers. But the moon was full and they all insisted on being allowed to wander. So I advised Mr. Harker to stay in his room that evening. If he needed to leave his room for any reason, I informed him, lingering anywhere else in the castle would be extremely unwise.

We then talked of other matters for some time before I left his room. I was worried about my three sisters of the night. Would they try to cause harm to Mr. Harker? Would the restless Englishman leave his room, despite my warnings? I decided the best way to keep the three sisters in check would be to provide them with their favorite meal.

In my rush to leave the castle, I did something unwise, considering the presence of an overly curious guest in the castle. I left through the window and crawled down the castle wall, face down. My fingers and toes grasped the corners of the stone, as well you know—I was the one who taught you how to creep along stone walls with the ease of any spider or lizard. Before I re-entered at a lower level, I happened to look up. I saw Mr. Harker staring down from his window, his eyes wide with horror.

I knew of a villager whose wife had recently birthed three fat babies. Too many mouths to feed for such an impoverished family. I decided to lighten their burden by a third.

None of my ladies were in their chambers when I returned from my errand. A burlap sack held dinner for them. Mr. Harker was also absent from his room. No doubt he was looking for a way out of the castle. I searched until I found the three hungry sisters in the dining hall, struggling with Mr. Harker.

I was having none of this. I pushed the three sisters away from Mr. Harker and gave them a stern warning. They were not to touch him or even look at him. They all backed away, pouting. One finally said, "Are we to have nothing tonight?" I pointed to the sack, which I had left by the door. Soon they were feasting with feverish delight.

I led Mr. Harker back to his room and locked him in. He was too tired and frightened to question me about what had happened. And I must say, I felt sorry for him. I used to be as he is: a man who fears darkness and death. He does not know what you and I know.

I unlocked his door closer to dawn. When evening came again, I met with him in the library. I told him that I wanted him to write three letters to both his fiancée and his employer, and date them June 12, June 19 and June 29. Considering the date, May 19, I am sure my request terrified the young solicitor.

A few nights later, a woman entered the courtyard, screaming, "Monster, give me back my child!" She was the mother of the child I had taken. She threw herself on her knees and raised up her hands. I whispered a summons into the darkness and soon, my wolves brought an end to her torment.

The next morning, as I rested in a box in the cellar—one of many special boxes—I was roused by a thunderous crash. Apparently the so-clever Mr. Harker had determined my location and kicked down the door to kill me. In that deep daytime slumber we both enjoy, I could dimly sense what was going on, but could not move. It was all like a dream to me. He used a shovel to pry at the lid of the box, and once it was open, he brough the shovel down upon my head. It makes me laugh, that he should think that feeble blow would kill me. He merely scratched me, and the wound healed in a moment. Mr. Harker must have been quite disappointed, to learn that his heroic gesture was such a foolish waste of time.

At that moment, a group of peasants who are loyal to me, like good hounds, entered the cellar. One of them threw Mr. Harker into a corner of the room, where he huddled, weeping like a child. They closed the lid of my box and loaded it, along with many other boxes, on the back of several horse-drawn carts. They were following instructions I had given them the night before. The bottom of each specially prepared box was loaded with the soil of our native land—soil that is still red with the blood of our enemies.

Following my plans, they loaded the boxes on a ship heading to England. Such a novel way to travel! I trust the hungry sisters entertained Mr. Harker in my absence, like good hostesses.

Please pay attention to the details of my travel in this letter. You may decide someday to move to America, a young and vibrant country. You might wish to use my methods to set up house there.

* * * *

My journey to Whitby, England, aboard the Russian schooner Demeter began on July 6th. On that day, we set sail from Varna into the Black Sea. On July 11th, we passed through the channel Bosphorus, which connects the Black Sea to the Sea of Marmora. The next day, we entered the Aegean Sea, and ten days later, we passed Gibraltar. On August 6th, we harbored in Whitby.

The first three days, I rested in my box in the hull of the ship. As I rested, I enjoyed blissful red dreams of what my new world will be like. I thought of all those tender, pale British fools. Their land does not know of those like us, my dove! Their homes will be my larders! So many pale throats—so much fresh blood!

And if they ever determined the nature of my existence—no matter. What can they do? They do not know of our kind. They will not know how to destroy me. I shall be invincible there.

Of course, my hunger could not lie dormant. After a pleasant rest, I thirsted for blood. At first I fed on the rats scurrying in the cargo bay. Filthy vermin, but I needed what little nourishment they could provide. but, such meager fare was like wrapping a sword slash with a single strip of cloth. I needed more blood, and preferably not from vile beasts. Their foul essence leaves a bitter taste in the mouth.

On July 9th, after the sun had set, I crept out of my box. A tall sailor was smoking a cigar starboard, gazing into the distance. I crept his way as quietly as a fog. Soon I was so close, I could smell the nauseating smoke from his cigar.

I grabbed him by the neck and put my other hand over his mouth, so he couldn't scream. Then I sank my fangs into his leathery neck and drank his delicious, robust blood. I was so famished, I drained him within minutes. When I was finished, I tossed his body overboard and returned to the box in the hull.

The sudden disappearance of the sailor frightened his shipmates. That same night, I could hear their nervous chatter from my hiding place. The next evening, I ventured forth once again, to see if I could find another lone sailor. To my dismay, there were several sailors keeping watch. I decided to bide my time. That, my dear, was an excellent decision. For those like us who can linger for centuries, it is always wise to rely on patience.

Night after night, I fed on the crew, singling them out one by one. The poor first mate, a nervous fellow, went quite mad. Driven insane by a shadowy figure, glimpsed from time to time! Soon there were only four crew members left, including the captain.

Still, I needed more time and opportunity to hunt before we reached England. One night, I scooped up two handfuls of soil from my box and tossed them together. A cloud of dust swirled through the hull—and through my will, I turned the cloud into a fog, a thick red fog that filled the cargo bay, staining the walls with fine red droplets. The fog crept up to the deck of the ship, clutching the vessel like a madman strangling his screaming victim. The sailors could not find their way to shore.

Then a violent storm broke—an unexpected but welcome addition to my plans. The captain strapped himself to the wheel with strong rope. The rain fell from the sky like a waterfall and the wind and waves rocked the boat furiously. I crept up behind the captain, and sank my fangs into his neck. So much rich, flavorful blood!

The schooner crashed ashore and drove up on the sand. Refreshed from my feast, I transformed into a gray wolf and sprang to the shore. I felt so deliciously liberated! I was finally off that floating prison of a boat. A new country filled with rich blood stretched before me.

In time, each night will be a glorious feast! But of course, I will first have to observe patience. I will need to befriend and charm the local people. Otherwise, they will immediately suspect the stranger in their midst when the deaths begin.

With love,
Father

* * * *

My little one,

As part of my travel plans, I had made arrangements for my boxes to my various properties across England upon their arrival. The rather spectacular appearance of the schooner brought more attention from the community than I would have wished, but eventually the thrill of it all passed from people's minds. That is the wonderful thing about mortals. They live only a short while, and their memories are so short. Such temporary creatures. But, that works in our favor. Time is our greatest ally. Clergy and other enemies may seek to destroy us, but eventually they age and die.

I have hired servants to clean and furnish Carfax Abbey during the day, while I sleep. I told them I was an author, and I did my best work at night. At least the second part of my claim is true. We both do our best work at night, do we not?

Perhaps I should become an author. How the world would tremble at the tales I could tell! I could fill many books with robust tales of warfare. These pale people of England, they would turn paler still if I should take the time to write an instructive essay on how best to impale one's victims. *Slowly,* of course!

Or, I could write about my occult studies. I could tell of my travels in Egypt, so very long ago. There I studied with the Cult of Nyarlathotep and learned how to extend my life forever by drinking fresh blood. I also learned to change my form, just as Nyarlathotep, the Crawling Chaos, can change into forms that humans might gaze upon without going mad.

Whenever my appetite for blood returns, I simply roam the countryside. It is easy enough to find farmers and hunters, tending to their tasks at hours when others have settled in for the night.

I have been meeting with many of the local families of prominence. After all the nourishment I have received, I feel much stronger. My hands are those of a fine young man, with none of the spots that come with age. I am sure many of the land-owners in this area are considering me as a possible husband for their plump, giggling daughters.

The people here in England are so class-conscious. Because I dress in the style of a distinguished gentleman, many of them fawn over me in a manner that is as lavish as it is ridiculous. Of course, they do not realize that despite my fanciful trappings, I am also a warrior. They would not coo and simper as they do, if they knew that I have pulled the intestines—and beating hearts!—from my screaming victims on the battlefield.

I have enjoyed several enjoyable visits with the Westenra family. The daughter, Miss Lucy, is quite lovely. She is so sweet, so lovely. I understand she has many gentlemen who are ardent admirers. With so many suitors, one might wonder if she is overly generous with her affections, but her scent is that of a virgin. How delightful! Soon, I know, she will be mine.

Already I can see that this venture is going to a marvelous success. After so many years of clinging to old ways, it is good to be moving in a new direction—a campaign of conquest.

With love,
Father

* * * *

My little one,

I have been visiting a patient in the nearby asylum. I drifted in through the barred window as mist, and the look on his face as I regained human form was quite amusing. He is a mentally weak man, easily influenced by my power. I can use such an ally. This Mr. Renfield, he has a most curious form of mania. He thinks that eating little living things will extend his life. I am encouraging his obsession. He will make an excellent servant.

I have also been visiting my lovely new friend, Miss Lucy. She has such lovely blonde locks and rosy pink cheeks. Absolutely enchanting! I found out that one of her suitors, Mr. Arthur Holmwood, has become her fiancé. That does not matter to me, of course. Also, it turns out that she socializes with Miss Mina Murray, the fiancée of Mr. Harker. I recently met Miss Mina at the Westenra house and she is quite charming.

I believe I mentioned in a previous letter that I had seen Miss Mina's image in a locket owned by Mr. Harker. At that time, I had noted her resemblance to both you and your beautiful mother Ilona. I shall be adding Miss Mina to my household after I have lured Miss Lucy into my embrace. That is good of me, yes? It would be awful for me to separate such loving friends! Also, with my many properties in England, they can help me to maintain them all. Miss Lucy and Miss Mina are both ladies of style. I am sure they would be able to add charm to my homes.

One night, I stood outside of Miss Lucy's home and summoned her. "My dear Lucy," I whispered. "Come to me. Come." It was a beautiful night with a bright, full moon in a sky resplendent with stars.

Within minutes, Miss Lucy appeared from out of the shadows. The girl was sleepwalking, her beautiful eyes staring at everything and nothing. I gently seated her on a nearby stone bench and untied the silk ribbons of her nightgown. I gazed upon her neck in the moonlight. I sat by her side and gently sank my fangs into her tender neck. Her blood was so pure, it was absolutely divine. I enjoyed her sweet essence as it trickled down throat.

A moment later, I felt another presence nearby. I looked up and saw Miss Mina approaching. She had not yet spotted us. She kept calling out, "Lucy! Lucy!"

I left Miss Lucy resting on the bench and disappeared into the night.

For two more nights, I tried unsuccessfully to drink Miss Lucy's sweet blood. Every time, Miss Mina thwarted my efforts. It was mid-August and the warm night was filled with brilliant moonlight. I turned into a bat and flew outside of Miss Lucy's window. The lovely but intrusive Miss Mina appeared at the window, looking out at me. I whirled in circles around the window, trying to catch a glance of my Lucy, but all I could see was Miss Mina.

A few nights later, I saw my dear ladies walking together shortly after nightfall. I hid in the shadows of the St. Mary's Church graveyard.

Suddenly Miss Lucy cried, "His red eyes again! They are just the same!" She pointed frantically in my direction. I disappeared into the darkness before Miss Mina could spot me.

Later that night, I hide outside of Miss Mina's bedroom. I hear her talking to Lucy. It seems she had received a letter from a Sister Agatha at the Hospital of St. Joseph and Mary in Budapest. Mr. Harker is being cared for at the Budapest hospital. He has been there for the last six weeks, suffering a violent brain fever. So! It would seem the three lovely sisters had to failed to exterminate him.

Miss Mina was packing to be with him. She mentioned that she was prepared to marry him as soon as humanly possible. How perfect! With her out of the country, I will be able to drink Miss Lucy's blood without interruption. Yes! I am determined to make Miss Lucy my new vampire bride.

While Miss Mina and Mr. Harker were entering matrimony, my fangs were once again entering Lucy's lovely neck. That week was filled with stormy weather, and each evening, I would scratch my nails on the glass to draw her to the window. I consumed more and more of Miss Lucy's life-force. At one point, I cut my wrist with my fangs and sprinkled a few glorious drops of my own blood into her eager mouth. My loving efforts are making her mine—mine forever!

I have been talking with Miss Lucy during my visits, and have learned that her pale complexion and weakness have become a concern of her fiancé. He took her to see Dr. John Seward, keeper of the nearby asylum. The physician examined her and apparently was baffled by her illness—as well he should be. What can this foolish medicine-man know of these matters?

Apparently Dr. Seward has written to a colleague, Dr. Van Helsing of Amsterdam, asking him to come to England to exam Lucy. This Dr. Van Helsing has ordered blood transfusions for Miss Lucy. So good of him to replenish my favorite source of nourishment! They can pour all the blood they want into her. It will all be mine.

These mortals—it is a delight to watch them stumble blindly through their mercifully short lives!

* * * *

I thought I had finished this letter—but, I never found the time to send it. Since then, more developments have arisen.

Apparently this Van Helsing fellow is smarter than I had guessed.

Last week, when I went to visit Miss Lucy, I found hideous garlic flowers piled around her window. When I scratched my nails on the glass, she came to the window with a wreath of the vile flowers draped around her neck. Of course I could not enter. I cannot bear the poisonous stench of those hideous blossoms! For the rest of that evening, I lingered outside the window, just out of sight. When Miss Lucy's mother entered the room, I listened to their conversation and learned that the flowers were part of Dr. Van Helsing's treatment.

I also learned that Miss Lucy's mother is already sick of the flowers and wishes to remove them. In every household, whatever the mother wants, the mother eventually gets. I need only to wait a short while and the flowers will be gone. And then, I will be able to finalize my plans for Miss Lucy and turn her into one of us.

It amazes me that this stupid doctor is trying to foil my plans. It is clear that he knows that people like us cannot stand garlic. He knows that much, but he does not know enough! If he knew enough, he would not try to stop me at all. He would be happy to know that I am trying to change Lucy. He would know that the new Lucy will be young, beautiful, enticing and powerful for ages to come! If he truly understood this, he would drag the girl to my feet and tilt back her head, offering me her graceful neck!

With love,
Father

* * * *

My little one,

I have been talking more with my insane friend Mr. Renfield. The poor creature would dearly love for me to make him immortal, but sadly, that will not be happening. I do not want a maniac following me like a hound for centuries. The hound might decide to bite his master. Even so, I am confident that I will be able to make use of him here in England.

I am happy to say that my patience was amply rewarded. After enough time without any disturbances, Miss Lucy's mother eventually removed the garlic flowers. That very night, I scratched my nails against the glass and Lucy let me in, breathing heavily with excitement.

After so long a wait for her delicious, virginal blood, I was exceedingly thirsty. Within minutes, I had drained Miss Lucy down to the last tantalizing drop. Just as I had finished my repast, a maid entered the room carrying fresh blankets. She dropped her burden and ran screaming out of the room. I followed her to the dining room, where another maid was dusting.

Both women turned toward me, their eyes wide with horror. It was easy enough to mesmerize them simply by staring at them. They fell to the floor as one, lost in a deep sleep. I had no complaint against them. There was no need for these simple servants to die.

I then heard a faint whimper from the corner of the room. I turned to the side and saw Miss Lucy's mother, huddled in the corner. She gazed up at me, tears streaming down her face. Her death would create even more chaos in the household, and chaos has always been my ally. I walked over to her, crouched by her side, and placed my hands around her throat. It took only a minute of steady pressure to extinguish her life.

I considered taking Miss Lucy to Carfax Abbey, but she would not be able to walk, and carrying her would certainly attract attention.

I am at Carfax Abbey now. No doubt the good doctors Van Helsing and Seward will stop by to see Miss Lucy in the morning. No doubt they will try a great many ridiculous measures to try to cure her, but there is nothing they can do now. She will only continue to change. They will say she is dying, but in fact, she is healing: recovering from the banal disease known as mortal life.

With love,
Father

* * * *

My little one,

My beatiful Lucy has passed away. Death has worked its magic on her and she has been transformed, wondrously transformed. She shall be hungry, wise and beautiful forever.

Last night, hours after her funeral, we walked through the cemetery together. How her pale hair glowed in the moonlight. Never before have her lips been so full and red. Ours is a joy that those weak, simple-minded mortals could never fathom. She shall be the first of many English brides, I am sure. The next one shall be Miss Mina.

I must keep this letter short, darling daughter. I have much to do! My next step is to crush all opposition, so that I can proceed with my plans without any obstacles. Very soon, I shall destroy all of my Lucy's suitors, as well as Mr. Harker and that pest Van Helsing.

Once I have tended to those trifling details, my existence here in England shall be filled with a profound joy I have not experienced in centuries.

With love,
Father

THE MOON IS OUR MOTHER

by Mark McLaughlin

The pale-eyed Mia-demon wandered through the ruined city, searching for amusement. But the hour was late and everyone she encountered was a poor prospect. The night's stragglers were either too old or too scrawny to bother with.

She scratched her lacquered claws against a brick wall. Where to look? The buildings around her were hopelessly dilapidated, with boarded windows and debris-choked entryways. And yet within.... secret gatherings? Strange couplings?

Most assuredly.

She walked toward a brick church spray-painted with graffiti. On the front steps, a pack of elderly streetpeople huddled around a small fire. They were all so filthy and diseased, she could hardly tell the men from the women. A fat, balding creature shifted and— What was this? From behind the behemoth peered a perfect young man, an angel nestled among trolls.

She wagged a finger at him, and a stupid, beautiful grin spread across his face.

An idiot. Intriguing.

The young man parted from the street creatures and the Mia-demon noticed that his gloves were pinned to his sleeves.

"That bitch means trouble," rasped the obese one to the angel-man. "There's a stick in front of you. Pick it up and hit her with it."

"Poke her eyes out!" one of the others shouted.

A brief look of worry crossed the young man's face. Then he picked up the stick, threw it at the fat troll and guffawed. "Shuddup or I'll poke you one!"

He lumbered to the Mia-demon and cocked his head. "You a devil?"

She nodded.

"That red hair's real purty. All you devils have red hair?"

She nodded again.

"Can't talk? Lemme see your mowf."

She stuck out her wriggling forked tongue. With a wink, she took him by the arm.

"So where we goin'?" He examined her opening, lingering on her sheer red blouse and snakeskin boots. Along the side of each boot was sewn a sheath. From these protruded slim handles of black wood.

* * * *

The demon led the angel-man down the street for several blocks. Soon they came to the burned-out husk of a pawnshop. An old white dog, half-sleeping, regarded them dreamily through the broken glass of a display case.

She motioned for the angel-man to throw a rock into the shop. He obliged, and threw in a few bricks as well.

A pale-eyed woman with crooked teeth entered the display case from the back of the shop. She squinted out at them, licking her lips. Her hair was a dark brownish-red. She wore dozens of necklaces— pearls, gold chains and lockets, all tangled together. Upon seeing the Mia-demon, she spat a thin stream of yellow venom. A few drops splashed on the dog's back. The animal yelped with pain and ran off into the night.

The woman inside the shop uttered a shrill hiss and crawled out onto the display, trying to keep her dog in sight. The Mia-demon pulled a dagger from her boot. She smiled as she threw the weapon, for she was glad to be rid of it. It silver blade wheeled and flashed.

Sorting through the gold necklaces around the throat of the snaggle-toothed woman, the Mia-demon found and removed a perfect string of pearls. The Mia-demon had always wanted a necklace like this, even in the old days when she'd worked in a place where slabs and slices of meat were cooked up for meals. Roasts, steaks—disgusting lumps of decay. And all that horrid silverware.

The angel-man found a decorative gold ring on the floor of the display. "Look at this, purty devil lady!" he said, slipping on the ring. "It's fancy! It's shaped like a big cat on a rock. You look like a big cat, too."

She regarded his angel's face affectionately. How very nice it was, to find someone so beautiful, so obedient….

* * * *

Under the skylight of an old warehouse, in a nest of yellowed newspapers, the demon and the idiot made love. The act did not take long. Upon completion, the Mia-demon raked a poisoned claw lightly across his chest and he fell asleep immediately. She did not tear into his chest and devour his living heart, as was her way. Instead, she removed a copper-bladed dagger from its sheath and sliced into her own wrist.

A ray of moonlight shot from the cut. She opened the angel-man's mouth and covered it with the incision. His cheeks glowed pale-blue. She looked up through the skylight at the moon. The round face of it flashed a bright blue scar—something alive and growing. nourished by the sun's energy.

It was said that one out of every six people turned demon under the blue light of the moon-chasm. The Mia-demon did not know why she was among those who changed. She only knew that when the moon was elsewhere, turning other lands into demon realms, her hair turned yellow and her tongue became a blunt slab. Afterward, the Mia-demon withdrew, leaving her Mia-self to wander, alone and frightened.

The demon pushed back one of the angel-man's eyelids. The moist orb was beginning to glow milky-blue. She tore a strip of fabric from her blouse and tied it around her wrist.

She left the warehouse and walked toward the church. The angel-man, she knew, would join her soon enough. In the distance, she heard cats fighting. Or mating? It was hard to tell the difference. She looked under her makeshift bandage at her wound. The cut was almost completely healed.

The huddled streetpeople were all asleep—except for one. A thin old woman in a tattered trenchcoat was keeping watch.

"You better be careful," the crone said. "That feller who took off with you, he loves us. He ain't gonna turn against us."

The demon stared hard into the old woman's eyes. And what sad brown eyes they were.

The old woman swallowed hard. "We raised him to do our work. We found him and he's ours."

The demon continued to stare.

The crone's voice grew softer. "The whole world's crazy. That moon's gonna be everybody's tombstone. You know that for sure." Her brown eyes rolled as she struggled to stay awake. "Them pearls you got there are like little moons. You know that? Just like little … moons. Just like … your eyes…."

The demon slid the copper dagger into the base of the sleeping crone's skull, slicing the spinal cord. One by one, she paralyzed the streetpeople as they slept. The task took less than a minute.

As soon as she was done, she heard the approach of quickening footsteps. She turned to see the angel-man leap toward her, his mouth gaping in a silent scream.

She kicked out, pushing him on his back. She tensed, expecting him to renew his attack. Instead, he scrambled toward her disabled victims.

He began to weep. His luminous tears glowed brightly on his cheeks. He struggled to speak, but failed.

Think to me. The Mia-demon concentrated, sending forth the strongest thought-voice she could muster. *We can understand each other now.*

Still crying, the angel-man tore into the obese woman's chest, the power of his inner glow compelling him to feast. The voice of his own thoughts was feeble and frightened. *They were my folks! This one was like my mommy. Purty soon they're all gonna be dead and it's your fault. You bad devil lady—I shouldn't a'let you touch me. You're not my mommy.*

The Mia-demon sighed. Even with blood on his lips, he had the face of an angel. And angels were meant to fall.

I can't be your mother, but I can be your sister. Would you like that? If you want to see our mother, just look up at the moon. Isn't it lovely? The moon is our mother. Say it! The moon is our mother.

The angel-man wiped away his tears. Blood drops fell from his chin. *The moon is our mother.*

The Mia-demon smiled. *Again. The moon is our mother.*

The idiot smiled back. *The mother is our mother. The moon is my mother. The moon is my mommy.*

DRACULA, INC.

by Michael McCarty

Lucy Brahms, the new red-haired administrative assistant at Dracula, Inc., watched with mingled fascination and repulsion as a strange coworker stood on the sofa, grab a spider off the wall, then popped most of it inside of his mouth. Four hairy legs protruded from his lips as he munched on his ghastly snack. At that moment, her boss spoke to her over the intercom.

"I am ready to see Mr. Renfield now," he said. His deep voide was wonderfully reassuring, settling the panic that was slowly rising in her.

"Yes, sir," she said. "I will send him in right away."

Mr. Renfield swallowed his juicy prey.

"Mr. Dracula will see you now," she said. She picked up her WORLD'S BEST SECRETARY mug and drank down the last of her coffee, wishing there was a shot of whiskey in it.

"Yes!" Renfield cried. He jumped from the couch and ran into the office, slamming the door behind him.

Dracula's office was incredibly huge. Its equipment and furnishings included ten scarlet filing cabinets, a computer, a combination copier and fax machine, a sofa, a bar, a refrigerator, an enormous U-shaped desk, and a large window that would have presented a marvelous view of the grounds of Dracula, Inc., if the glass hadn't been coated with a light-proof membrane of black plastic.

"Please, Mr. Renfield," Dracula said softly, "have a seat."

Renfield looked at the chair in front of him and jumped up and down with excitement. "An excellent idea, Master! A new seat for my office! My old wooden chair is very uncomfortable and this nice padded seat is so much better. You are so smart, Master!"

Dracula sighed and rolled his bloodshot green eyes. "I meant, sit down. Please sit down."

"Yes! Another excellent idea, Master!" Renfield said, quickly sitting down.

"Please, just call me Dracula. People in America do not call their superiors 'Master.'"

"Yes, Master," Renfield covered his mouth with thin, trembling fingers. "Sorry! I meant 'Mister.' Mister…"

"Dracula." The vampire smiled. "Call me Mister Dracula. That is preferable to Master, Vlad the Impaler, or Prince of Darkness."

"Yes, Mister Dracula."

"Much better. I understand that you may be nervous. Annual job reviews aren't much fun. I appreciate the honesty and enthusiasm expressed in the self-evaluation forms you completed yesterday. Nevertheless, you do need to hear some straight talk from your boss."

"Thank you, Ma—" Renfield covered his mouth, took a deep breath, and then said, "Mister Dracula. Please continue."

Dracula picked up and perused a printed form. "Now let's see… I needed to rate your performance in the categories of Quality of Work, Days Missed, Attitude, and Late Arrival. As far as Quality of Work goes, I rated you, 'Average: makes occasional mistakes.' Your biggest mistake was leading Dr. Van Helsing to the headquarters. But, that was dealt with."

"I'm sure sorry about that one," Renfield said, bowing his head in shame.

"No harm done," Dracula said, waving his hand. "Van Helsing has been a thorn in my side for years. I always manage to send him off on some wild goose chase." He glanced at the paper again. "Next topic: Days Missed. Let's talk about sick leave. You had used two-hundred hours of sick leave last year. A little high. But, it was because you were confined to the state mental hospital, so we'll allow it."

Renfield nodded eagerly in agreement.

Dracula continued the evaluation. "Attitude. That's a tough one for you. You're usually extremely agreeable, but you don't always accept constructive supervision. For example, two months ago, I made some suggestions about how to increase your productivity and you tried to stake me."

"I'm sorry about that, too," Renfield said, a tear rolling down his cheek. "I lost my temper. I shouldn't have tried to put a wooden stake through your heart. My bad."

"And you promise not to bring stakes into the office again…?"

"No more stakes. I promise."

"Now, we need to address the issue of Late Arrival. You have been tardy twenty-two times in the last year. As cited in the Dracula, Inc. handbook on page seven: 'An employee is to be at work at or before the exact starting time for his/her position.' Your starting time is 9:00 a.m. But during those times you were tardy, you were chasing or eating a pest, be it a spider, cockroach, rat or whatever. Because of your vermin-eating habit, you have saved the company many thousands of dollars in extermination fees. So, let's never worry about tardiness."

"Thank you, Ma—Mister Dracula."

"Overall rating: Very good. Positive impact on operations. Clearly insane, occasionally homicidal, but a hard worker and very loyal—which is almost a lost art these days. Great multi-tasker—you do your job well, keeping projects in order, eating pests and spying on other employees, all at the same time. Friendly and easy to work with … most of the time. Plus, you were a blast at the staff Halloween party last year, when you got drunk and tried to dance—you were stiffer than Frankenstein's monster! Your performance was downloaded on the company website and still receives thousands of hits."

"Yeah…" he said, blushing. "Frankenstein's monster isn't the only one with two left feet."

Dracula grinned broadly, revealing his gleaming eye-teeth. "In conclusion, I say this: Mr. Renfield, you're a hell of a worker, so I'm giving you a big raise this year."

"Thank you, Master—um, *Mister* Dracula!" Renfield jumped out of his chair and started shaking the cold, long-nailed hand of his boss.

"You're welcome. Oh, before you leave the room … a big cockroach just scurried behind the refrigerator. Could you take care of that? Thanks!"

SCRAWNY GOON IN DARK GLASSES

by Mark McLaughlin

Odelia couldn't help but wonder why that pale, scrawny goon always wore dark glasses. It couldn't be for the fashion—his clothes and haircut were god-awful. Maybe there was something wrong with his eyes. She once read an article in one of the tabloids about some guy with a problem like that: MOLE BOY DOOMED TO LIFE IN DARKNESS.

She couldn't figure out the scrawny goon's age. He was gangly in a teenish sort of way, but he also had quite a bit of stubble. And his skin looked coarse … unhealthy. She guessed that he was probably in his early twenties.

Maybe he was a college student. That would explain why he was always here in the library. The funny thing was, he never checked anything out. He just seemed to wander, picking up books and rifling through them.

Odelia pulled a weak smile. What would Henry say if he knew that she spent this much time thinking about another man? A fifty-year-old mother of two, gawlign after a complete stranger. Then something else occurred to her. What if the Director caught her lollygagging like this? She'd probably be the first volunteer ever to be dismissed.

She looked around to see if the Director was watching. She couldn't see him—maybe she should check to see if he was in his office….

….*and there I go,* Odelia thought, *worrying over something stupid.*

Always fretting. Always agonizing about what others thought, That was what had ruined his last two jobs, both with insurance companies. She hadn't been able to concentrate. Relatively innocuous comments from her co-workers set her on edge. As a result, too many errors and oversights found their way into her work.

And now her she was, doing volunteer work to fill her days. Henry had thought the library would help her to regain her confidence. If anything, she felt more worthless than ever before.

Odelia's foot skidded on something soft. She almost fell, but she caught herself in time. Part of a sandwich—now there was peanut butter smeared on the carpet. Why did people insist on bringing food into the library? Why did they go to all the bother of packing it up, smuggling it in, and hiding in the stacks to eat it? And if they absolutely had to chow down, couldn't they at least clean up their own mess?

Odelia went to the storage room and filled a bucket with soapy water. After some searching, she dug up a sponge and a firm brush. She wasn't going to bother asking the janitor to clean up that mess. He wouldn't get to it for hours, and in the meantime, more people might walk through it, tracking peanut butter everywhere.

Of course, it seemed like whenever there was a mess to be found, she was the one to find it. She was the one who'd found that poor old woman last month. Dead of a heart attack. That was the day she'd first noticed the scrawny goon in dark glasses.

Walking past the staff lounge, she thought about grabbing a snack. But no, a candy bar was the last thing she needed. Her parents used to say she was big-boned. Over the years, those big bones had picked up more padding than she cared to admit.

A sudden movement by the baseboard caught her eye. She kicked out and crushed a cockroach against the wall.

As she returned to the mess with her bucket and sponge, she noticed someone crouched over the remains of the sandwich. The scrawny goon in dark glasses. He looked up at her, smiled, and moved a few feet away.

Odelia sponged away at the carpet. Just what had that strange man been doing? It looked like he was about to pick up that dirty, trod-upon sandwich. Was he going to throw it away, or was he going to *eat* it?

She glanced up at him. His clothes certainly needed washing. Maybe he was some hungry streetperson. Or maybe a junkie. Didn't she read somewhere that people who took drugs always wore dark glasses?

Odelia finished cleaning the carpet and returned the bucket and sponge to the storage room. While she was there, she found a marker and a sheet of paper and made a sign: NO FOOD OR DRINK AL-LOWED.

As she pinned her sign to the message board near the entrance, she noticed the scrawny goon staring at her, or at least in her direction. It was so hard to tell.

She walked to the water fountain, and he turned his head to follow her. So he *was* watching her. Maybe he was planning on robbing her. Wasn't that how junkies got their drug money, by robbing people? Not now, but later, while she was walking to her car. She had some pepper spray in her purse, and what was that one trick she'd read about? Holding the car keys so that they stuck out between your fingers, like spikes? She would have to keep that in mind.

* * * *

As she reshelved books, Odelia thought about what sort of job she should apply for next. Nothing with typing, that was for sure. Maybe a daycare center. No, raising her own children had pretty much burned out her maternal instinct.

Whatever she picked, it would have to be something interesting. Something results-oriented. Something that would take her mind off her worries.

If only she had gone to college, instead of marrying Henry straight out of high schools. It seemed like all the really good jobs required a degree. Going back to school was out of the question. They could never afford it. Tonight she would look through the classifieds again and see if anything caught her eye.

Later that day she saw the man in dark glasses walking through the children's section. He was looking down the stacks as though searching for something. He stopped for a moment, smiled, then continued.

Where he stopped....

Last week, a little boy had been found unconscious in that aisle. Odelia's guess was that he'd suffered a seizure of some sort. He had awakened just as the paramedics were putting him on the stretcher. She could still remember his eyes: no spark, no expression. Completely soulless.

A teenage girl with braces asked for help in finding books on insects. Paula was tempted to tell her to go home and look them up on the internet—but no, she wasn't there to discourage library use. She ended up tracking down a half-dozen books for the girl, who took two without even thanking her.

Odelia wrinkled her nose as she returned the rest of the books to their shelves. Bugs. Why in the world did God make bugs so incredibly ugly? All those legs and wings and mandibles. And didn't they lay about five-thousand eggs at a time? Monsters, that's what they were.

She noticed that the scrawny goon in dark glasses had moved on to the reference section. What was that he was reading? A phone book?

Now he was staring at her again. Staring and smiling. Maybe he was looking *her* up in the phone book. Of course, he didn't know her name. Or did he…? At some point, he might have noticed her name tag: ODELIA JONES, VOLUNTEER—MAY I HELP YOU? God, she'd been so proud when they'd given her that name tag!

There I go again, she thought. *Worrying like an idiot.*

He seemed to be absorbed in the book now. Odelia moved to the side, then approached him from an angle. She hated herself for being so paranoid, and yet she couldn't help it. She had to see what the Hell a guy like that could find so interesting in a phone book.

In a moment, she was a few feet behind him. She suddenly felt very aware of the size of her body. She moved closer to the scrawny goon and leaned forward, hoping to catch a glimpse of the book. If he noticed her, she could pretend she was reaching for one of the other books near him.

He appeared to be looking at the map section of the phone book. Suddenly he closed the book, turned around and stumbled into her.

She grabbed his arm to steady herself, but he was too light to support her. She pulled him down as she fell, knocking off his glasses in the process. She looked up and realized he was staring straight at her—

—with eyes like black whirlpools, drawing her in. She found herself being chased through a shadowed, cobweb-strewn version of the library. Her pursuer was the scrawny goon in dark glasses, but here he was different: part man, part spider. His deformed face and tal-

oned hands were covered with thick, glistening black fur. Her heart was pounding so hard, she worried that she was minutes from a heart attack. She raced among the stacks, through greasy webwork that stuck to her hair and clothes. His claws fastened on her shoulder and turned her around. His mouth began to writhe and froth, blossoming like a hideous flower with toothy petals—

—and suddenly Odelia was back where she had fallen, too breathless to scream. The reference librarian had returned the dark glasses to the nameless man. His eyes were hidden now. He scrambled to his feet and rushed off.

Odelia got up and followed him out of the building. The streets were busy, but she managed to keep him in view, following him across the street and around a corner. She trailed him up the street for a few blocks, then suddenly down an alley. There he slipped on a trash can lid and twisted his ankle.

This gave her the half-minute she needed to catch up with him.

As she picked up the brick, she felt … for the first time in her life … actually happy to be a big woman. A big, strong woman.

That evening, she asked Henry to pass the classifieds.

The listings under Pest Control intrigued her.

INCIDENT IN THE BACK OF A BLACK LIMOUSINE

by Michael McCarty & Mark McLaughlin

"The darkness will swallow you into the belly of the night...."

Van Helsing turned around to see the person talking to him. It was a tall, thin man, standing in the shadows of a nearby alley. From what he could make out, the man carried a walking stick and wore a top hat, a long duster, and black cowboy boots ... an odd combination of formal and casual attire. Van Helsing tightened his hold on his black leather satchel.

"That's why it's so important not to spend the night alone," added the tall man.

Gray-haired Van Helsing nodded. "Agreed. But my wife passed away many years ago. Good evening, young man."

"Young...?" The tall man chuckled. "How amusing." He stepped out of the shadows. He was a handsome fellow, with a well-groomed black moustache, bright green eyes and an inviting smile. The light of the full moon gave his pale complexion a shine like polished aluminum. All of his clothes were black except for his top hat, which was maroon. He wore several black, red and silver medals on his duster. They looked foreign to Van Helsing, like artifacts from some distant country.

"They call me Big Daddy," he said, extending his hand.

The gray-haired man shook the stranger's hand and found it to be disturbingly cold and dry. "Van Helsing."

"As I was saying, Mr. Van Helsing ... you don't have to spend the night alone. I have some colleagues I think you might like to meet. *Lovely* young colleagues."

"Lovely, you say...?" Van Helsing laughed softly. "I will admit, it's been some time since..." His voice trailed off when he caught a glimpse of pointed teeth in Big Daddy's smile. After a moment's pause, he continued. "Now where were we? Oh, yes. Lovely. No harm in meeting some young lovelies, I suppose! Are they nearby?"

"Not too far. Come with me, please." So saying, Big Daddy passed him and walked down the street.

Van Helsing tugged his satchel under his arm and followed.

Big Daddy led him to a railroad bridge overpass. He stopped under the bridge, waiting for Van Helsing to catch up. The gray-haired man noticed that numerous inverted crosses of various colors had been spray-painted on the supports of the bridge.

Big Daddy followed his gaze. "Interesting, aren't they?"

"I imagine this is a meeting place for worshipers of evil … if one believes in that sort of thing," Van Helsing said. "Friends of yours, perhaps?"

"Could be," Big Daddy said with a shrug. "I have lots of friends. What they do in their spare time is no concern of mine. I'm too busy tending to my customers."

Van Helsing considered the statement. "Does that mean your customers aren't your friends?"

"My customers are temporary acquaintances," Big Daddy said, "and I always make sure they get what they paid for."

After passing under the bridge, they walked down a dark side street. Most of the streetlights were busted or burned out, making it difficult for Van Helsing to make out most of his surroundings. But there was one thing up ahead that was easy to see—a black stretch limousine, parked next to a blazing trashcan fire.

Big Daddy quickened his pace as he approached the limousine. "Right this way," he said as he opened the back door. "Welcome to my parlor, said the spider to the fly." Van Helsing chuckled as he entered the luxury car. Big Daddy had to remove his hat before joining him inside.

The first thing Van Helsing noticed upon entering the limousine was that they weren't alone. Across from him sat a lovely redhead, scantily clad in scarlet lingerie. Next to her sat a brunette draped in a silky black peignoir. Both women were slender and pale, with green eyes and painted red lips.

"These are the lovely young colleagues I mentioned," Big Daddy said. "The red-hot redhead is Lucy and the saucy brunette is Mina."

Both girls giggled at the same time, their bright eyes flashing. Van Helsing wondered if they were on drugs.

"Our driver this evening—every evening, in fact!—is my assistant, Renfield." Big Daddy leaned forward and tapped on the dark glass that separated the driver from his passengers. "Say hello, Renfield."

The dark glass slid down, revealing a pale, dark-haired young man with a spotty complexion and deep-set brown eyes, glazed with boredom. "Yo," Renfield said, turning back to his porn magazine.

"Since this is Wednesday," Big Daddy said to the gray-haired man, "I will give you a midweek discount... the Hump Day Special. You can have both girls for one price." He then whispered the amount into Van Helsing's ear.

"Good Lord!" Van Helsing said upon hearing the quote. "That's what I spend on a month's groceries!"

"One night of carnal pleasure with Lucy and Mina is worth far more than thirty nights of lunch meat and cheap beer," Big Daddy said, matter-of-factly.

"Sure, but I still have to eat," Van Helsing said. "At any rate, I'm not interested in the girls. I'm more interested in you."

"Me?" Big Daddy said, raising an eyebrow. "Sorry, but no. My role in the flesh-for fantasy business is managerial. Still, if you're looking for a young gentleman's company, I'm sure Renfield would be happy to oblige."

"Not like I have anything else to do," the driver said.

"I'm not interested in that, either," stated the gray-haired man. "I just want to talk with you."

"Talk...?" Big Daddy thought for a moment. "They say talk is cheap ... but not around here."

Van Helsing fished a fifty out of his pocket. "I'm not a rich man. Will this do?"

"I can give you a few minutes." Big Daddy plucked the bill from between Van Helsing's fingers. "Girls, Renfield ... go wait by the fire, please."

The girls and the driver promptly vacated the vehicle.

"It's good that you said 'please,' Big Daddy. It shows that you care."

"Thank you. I try. So what did you want to talk about, Mr. Van Helsing?"

The gray-haired man pulled the satchel from under his arm.

"Actually, it's *Sergeant* Van Helsing," he said, pulling a badge and a pistol out of his work case. "And, you are under arrest." He then informed Big Daddy of his rights.

"Aren't you way too old to be a cop?" asked the pallid pimp.

Van Helsing pouted. "I'm only fifty-seven. My sister keeps telling me I should dye my hair."

"Wouldn't hurt."

"I've been watching you for quite a long time," the policeman said. "I know who you are and more importantly, *what* you are: Big Daddy Dracula, the Pimp of Darkness. I just have one question, before I take you in."

"What's that?"

"How did you end up here in Scranton, Pennsylvania? You used to have a castle in the Carpathian Mountains! Now you're a flesh peddler in a Middle Colony state. What happened?"

Dracula sighed. "It's a long, sad tale … an epic tragedy."

Van Helsing nodded. "Give me the condensed version."

"In the old days, I was a great soldier … a warrior-king," Dracula said. "The engine of my power was fueled by gore. The ground was red with the life-force of my enemies. The magic of blood kept me young throughout the centuries … I'm as strong as a hundred men!

"But I didn't keep up with the rest of the world. I'm an antique … a quaint living fossil. I don't understand today's technology and I can't go out in the day, so I have to do what I can, just to keep moving forward. Carnage, I understand…and lust, too. I can't be a soldier—not with today's technology—but at least I can be a flesh merchant. There's money in it, and some prestige, too. The occupation of pimp is the best I can do these days. But at least I still have the magic. The magic of the blood stored within me—"

"That's all well and good," Van Helsing said, "but it has nothing to do with me. I still have to take you downtown."

The vampire smiled at the police officer, revealing his sharp fangs. "So Sergeant Van Helsing … how exactly do you plan to take me downtown with you? Slap the cuffs on me and march me through the night like some downtrodden punk-ass bitch?"

"I have a cellphone," the policeman said. "I'm going to call for backup in a minute, okay? You'd better cooperate, if you know what's good for you. This gun has silver bullets in it, and they've all been blessed by a priest. I also have a wooden stake in my satchel. And garlic. And a little bottle of holy water."

"I see. Clearly you've done your research." The vampire sighed again. "Fine. Cuff me." He held out his hands.

Van Helsing pulled the cuffs out of his satchel. "Actually, these go behind your back. It would be easier if we stepped outside."

"Renfield and the girls are out there. Not in front of the help, please. Let me keep my dignity."

"Well, let's see. This limousine's roomy enough… Okay, turn around as best you can and put your hands behind your back. That ought to do it."

The vampire turned away from Van Helsing and put his hands behind his back. It took some doing, but the policeman managed to fastened the cuffs while still holding the gun on the vampire.

However, he hadn't taken into consideration the vampire's incredible strength.

Dracula snapped the chain of the handcuffs as easily as a child snapping a daisy chain. He whipped around, swept away the satchel, and pounced upon the policeman, knocking him back on the seat cushions. The gun flew out of the policeman's hands.

Van Helsing quickly pulled out the silver cross hanging around his neck. The vampire edged away from him, shielding his eyes and hissing.

The policeman knew he had only seconds. He looked around but could not see the gun or the satchel. He grabbed the vampire's walking stick, snapped it in half, and rammed a jagged shard of wood into the vampire's heart. Black, rotted blood gushed from the wound like filth from a broken sewer pipe. He had to shield his face so that the stinking fluid didn't splash in his eyes and mouth.

Suddenly he heard the loud *click* of the limousine's doors locking. The blood continued to flow and flow from the vampire's chest.

"What's going on?" Van Helsing cried. "So much blood! Why?"

The vampire laughed—the merry howl of a dying demon. "It's all here, Van Helsing! All the blood I've ever sucked down in my life! Gallons, endless gallons! You've released the magic, and here it is! All of it! *All for you!*"

"No—that's insane! Let me out of here!" Van Helsing pounded at the windows of the limousine, but didn't have enough strength to shatter them. He couldn't find any window controls on the door or the roof of this luxury death chamber.

The back of the limousine was now half-full of black, slimy blood—and still, more and more kept pouring out of the vampire's body. Dracula's eyes blazed like twin green beacons.

The policeman pulled the wooden shard out of the vampire's body, thinking that might somehow the fix this impossible situation. But, it only made matters worse. The blood gushed out of the body like a high-pressure torrent from a fire hose.

Within seconds, Van Helsing found himself swallowed by darkness—completely surrounded by creamy magical gore. With his last scream, the air left his body and the vampire's timeless supply of blood filled his lungs.

VENUS

by Mark McLaughlin

Richard and Tyler were having lattes at the Books & Beans bookstore and coffee shop when they noticed Venus.

The young men were talking about a brochure they'd worked on earlier that day. They were both part of the Marketing and Public Relations department of a four-hospital health care system. They heard a dainty cough by the counter, and turned in unison.

The woman at the counter gave them a polite smile… One that seemed to say, *I didn't mean to attract your attention, so please turn away.* She was probably about six feet tall, but very thin, pale and fine-boned. Her eyes were hidden behind midnight-blue sunglasses, and her lipstick was a deep maroon. She had braided her long, shining black hair and artfully piled it atop her head. Two chopsticks and a few gold clips held the coiffure in place. She wore a black velvet dress that looked more like a jacket that had been made way too long, with a gold zipper that ran from her cleavage to her knees. Black high-heels and a large, black leather handbag completed the look.

She took her oolong tea and almond biscotti to a table in a far corner of the coffee shop, where she began to read a magazine somebody had left behind.

"Look at her," Richard said. He was a thin, red-haired man who had a habit of chewing on his lower lip. "Bet she's some kind of socialite."

"Then why would she come here?" Tyler asked. "Besides, she's too gorgeous to be some stuck-up society gal. Look at her. She's a goddess. A regular Venus." He was stocky, with blond hair and apple cheeks.

Richard shook his head and smiled. "You always have to do me one better, don't you?"

"What do you mean?"

"Well, I called her a socialite, so of course, you have to call her something on an epic scale—Venus!"

Tyler shrugged. "Just making small talk. And what do you mean, 'always'?"

"Well, like at work." Richard hooked a thumb west—their workplace was about four miles in that direction. "In the staff meeting, I started talking about how we could put the community newsletter on the website as a pdf file. So right away, you launched into how we could put the company newsletter on the employee intranet, too. I was going to get to that, but you stole my thunder."

"How should I know?" Tyler said. "I thought we were brainstorming. Oh geez…" He lowered his voice. "Look what's coming in. Now we're gonna have to listen to all *that*."

A sunburned, heavyset woman in a plain yellow dress strolled into the shop, shooing three noisy, bickering little girls ahead of her. "Keep movin', don't get in Mama's way. Missy, leave Mindy alone. Stop that. Find a table while Mama gets her coffee."

Richard sighed. "Coffee shops shouldn't allow in anyone under twelve."

"Make that eight." Tyler winced. "I did it again, didn't I?"

The girls settled on a table near Venus. "My name is Millie," one little girl said to the thin, dark-haired woman. "What's yours?"

Venus gave the child a bored, mildly amused smile. "Mercedes."

"It starts with an 'M'!" the child shrilled. "You could be my sister!"

The thin woman's smile turned hard. "Unlikely."

The mother, coffee cup in hand, went to join her children. She was standing next to Venus' table when the girl grabbed her by the elbow. "Mommy, this lady's name—"

The child's tugging caused her mother to drop the cup on Venus's table. Hot coffee splashed on the women and children, and shards of broken cup scattered around the shop.

Instantly the two men rushed to help Venus. Two clerks ran to the mother's assistance. The children began to scream at top volume.

"That clumsy, stupid cow!" hissed the thin woman. "I just bought this dress!"

Richard dabbed at her outfit with a handful of paper napkins. Suddenly he realized that he was, in effect, patting her bosom.

"Get your paws off me, you filthy cretin!" she cried.

"I wasn't—! Really, I was just…I mean…" His face turned rose-red.

"Hey, he was only trying to help," Tyler said. "Don't freak out, okay?"

"He can help those little idiots," she said. "Those three squealing monsters!"

A middle-aged woman with tortoise-shell glasses came running out of a back room. "Oh, dear. I heard some noise. I'm the manager—is there anything I can do?"

"Call your lawyer, you buffoon," Venus said. "I'm completely scalded! I am going to sue this dump back to the Stone Age."

"Honey, the coffee wasn't *that* hot," the mother said.

"Don't call me 'Honey', you ridiculous bucket of lard!" the thin woman cried.

"Jesus Christ, lady!" Tyler said. "So somebody spilled some coffee on you. That doesn't mean you have to act like a weirdo, calling people names and getting all bent out of shape. Lighten up already!"

"Yeah," the mother said. "Lighten up, you scrawny bitch. See, I can call people names, too! Anybody can do it."

One little girl stared looked up at their mother. "Mommy! You said a swear!"

The adults turned to Venus, waiting to see how she would respond to the mother's words.

The thin woman suddenly looked down. "My *bag!*" she whispered. Then, louder, she said, "What has happened to my bag?"

The adults began looking under tables.

"I only see two children," Venus said. "One of those awful little thieves has my bag!"

"Missy is probably just playing with it somewhere. She likes purses, that's all," the mother said. "She has five little toy purses at home. She's no thief! She's only six!"

Venus brushed past the men, out of the coffee shop and into the larger bookstore section of the business. She hurried through the aisles, looking for the child and her bag.

Tyler turned to his friend. "We should just go."

Richard smiled. "No, I want to see what happens." He walked into the bookstore area, chewing his lower lip. He watched Venus as she searched.

The mother and her two remaining children began to search as well. All of their clothes were spattered with coffee.

"You aren't thinking of asking that loony bitch out, are you?" Tyler said. "She's crazy. Nuts. I think she's got some kind of rage disorder."

"Oh, I don't know," Richard replied. "She'd just been splashed with hot coffee. That would make anyone blow up. Besides, maybe I like crazy girls."

"That's true," Tyler said, nodding. "You used to go out with Linda. And Simone. And what's-her-name with the tattoo…" Suddenly he pointed across the store. "Hey, look. Venus is heading for the children's section. I bet that's where the kid went."

Richard walked across the store, Tyler following close behind. Soon they'd caught up with the thin woman.

She stopped and stared at them. "Well if it isn't the groper and the loudmouth. Why are you two following me?"

Richard stepped up to her. "You look like you could use some help." He jerked his head toward Tyler. "Plus, my friend didn't mean to offend you."

"Oh. Yeah." Tyler managed the best apologetic smile he could. "Hot coffee splashing out of nowhere, that would upset anyone."

Venus sighed hugely. "Very well then. Help me find my bag. Please. I just want to get it back and go home."

The mother and her daughters hurried over to them. "Lady," the heavyset woman said, "I don't want to get into a screaming match with you. I'm just worried about my Missy. Did you have anything dangerous in that purse of yours? Any sleeping pills or pepper spray or… Oh Lord, I hope you didn't have a gun in there."

Venus made a face that Richard found impossible to interpret. Her eyebrows shot up and the corners of her mouth turned downward.

"I think," the thin woman said, "we should concentrate on finding the girl. I'm going to check the children's section." She turned to do so, and that put her in view of a plate glass window. "There! Out in the parking lot! What in the world is she doing?"

The little girl was out in the lot crawling on her hands and knees, with the bag on her back.

"She's playing camel. She saw a movie with a camel in it a couple nights ago." The mother walked over to the glass and rapped on it. "Missy!" she yelled. "Stop that! Cars can't see you when you're down that low!"

Richard, Tyler and Venus all ran out of the store, followed by the mother and the two girls.

Richard spotted the girl, who was now standing up, and ran over to her. The bag was nowhere to be seen. "Little girl," he said. "You had a black bag a moment ago. Where did it go?"

Missy pouted. "A mean man grabbed my camel hump. He went *that* way." She pointed to a restaurant on the other side of the parking lot. A man in a red sweater ran behind the building.

"My bag!" Venus cried as she hurried across the lot.

"Now what?" Tyler said.

Richard shrugged. "Follow her, I guess." He turned toward the mother. "Are you all okay?"

"We're fine, thanks," the heavyset woman said. "Go help the skinny bitch. I mean, lady. Come on, girls, let's go get some ice cream."

The two men ran toward the restaurant—Colonel Smiley's Family Fun Goodtime Eats. They saw Venus dodge behind the building.

"You've got to admit," Richard said, panting, "she's got guts, tearing after a purse-snatcher like that. He's probably a desperate criminal."

"We should've told that big gal to call the cops." Tyler said. "Hell, *we* should be calling the cops."

Richard stopped just as he reached the corner of the building. "That's not a bad idea. I'll just make sure he's not trying to kill her or something…"

He popped his head around the corner for a quick peek. But he didn't pull his head back. He just kept on looking.

So Tyler looked around the corner, too.

The area behind the restaurant was a small lot for employee parking, with a dumpster on one side and crates piled against the wall. The purse-snatcher was on his back, writhing in the middle of the lot as he was being attacked. But not by Venus. She was simply standing over him with her hands on her hips.

The thing attacking the man was—

The bag.

Its strap, a black, shiny tentacle, was wrapped firmly around the man's throat so he couldn't scream. Two side pockets had opened up, revealing glowing, bluish-green eyes. The main compartment of the bag didn't contain lipsticks, combs, tissues or even a checkbook. But it did contain plenty of teeth. Long, thin, yellowed teeth, like old ivory knitting needles. These tore into the purse-snatcher again and again, ripping through his skin, flinging out organs and blood-soaked loops of intestines.

Venus happened to look up.

She gave the boys a crooked smile and pulled down on the zipper of her dress.

Beneath the black velvet was…more black, but not velvet. Beneath her perfect snow-white breasts, the skin of her lower thorax matched her handbag. Two thin vertical lips stretched the length of her belly. As she began to walk toward them, the lips opened, revealing teeth like those of the bag. But hers were longer, and crooked, and they gnashed furiously, spraying forth ribbons of bubbling saliva.

She certainly had the body of a Venus.

A Venus flytrap, that is.

Richard and Tyler both uttered high yips of panic and ran back toward the bookstore parking lot.

"Oh my God, where's your car, your car, where's your God-damned *car?*" Tyler shouted.

"There, by that blue van!"

The two men hurried into Richard's little silver hatchback and raced off.

They didn't say anything for the next two minutes. Both were fish-belly pale and streaming with sweat.

Finally Tyler said, "I'll try not to steal your thunder in meetings, okay? Okay?"

"What…? Oh, that? Sure, that's fine. I'm not worried about it." Richard drove on, chewing frantically at his lip.

"Where are you going?" Tyler said.

"I—I'm not sure." He looked around. "There's a hotel—it's gotta have a bar. You want to go get a drink? A drink sounds really good right about now."

"Yes. God, yes."

As they pulled into a parking space in the hotel lot, Tyler said with a nervous laugh, "So, dude—I think she likes you! You gonna ask her out?"

"Hell, no!" Richard laughed, too—a high-pitched, frantic cackle. "She has a kid. I bet his name is—Percy!" He continued to laugh and laugh and laugh, tears trickling down his face, until the laughter turned to screams.

WANTED: UNDEAD OR ALIVE

by Michael McCarty

I'd been tracking the vampire for four nights. Riding through the desert, town to town, searching caves along the way. Wherever he went, I followed, which isn't as easy as it sounds. If you're too close, he'll smell your scent and if you're too far away, you'll lose him in the darkness.

Four nights of dust, tumbleweeds and the howls of coyotes in the distance. This particular night, I was on top of a hill, watching him in the valley below. He was at an encampment, a covered wagon and a campfire. One by one, he was draining the family there dry—a father, a mother and their boy.

I'd decided to wait until he was nearly finished before moving in. That way, he would be so bloated with blood, he'd barely be able to lift a finger, let alone escape. He'd already fed upon the father and the boy. When I finally approached the camp, he was sucking the last drops of blood out of the mother. Tortured and drained of her body fluids, she looked like a broken scarecrow during a drought.

Up close, the undead creature looked even more hideous with his fishbelly-white skin, ragged bloodstained nails, razor-sharp fangs, and eyes like polished tin. I didn't dare to look directly into those eyes. I'd done my research and legends say, his kind can mesmerize you like a serpent before the strike.

"A boy!" he cackled.

I pulled my gun out of my holster—a Colt Single Action Army, also known as the Peacekeeper.

"Such a big gun for one so small," the creature said with a smirk.

I tried not to show any fear. I knew he could sense fear like a hungry wolf sniffing around bleating sheep.

"So, little one. What's your name?" he said.

"Blake," I said. My mouth felt as dry as the mother's corpse looked. "Blake Sheldon, mister." I try to be polite, but I wasn't about to call this monster 'sir'.

"So, little Blake Sheldon. How old are you?"

"Old enough to kill ya."

"Touché. What does that make you...fifteen years old?"

"Sixteen. Almost seventeen."

"That's just a blink of the eye for me," he said. "And speaking of eyes, you need to look me in the eye when you talk to me, boy."

"I don't 'need' anything a leech like you has to offer," I said, trying my best to sound brave. "You killed my mother and father. Now I'm going to kill you."

"You don't say." He flashed a huge grin, revealing more of his sharp, blood-streaked teeth. "I bet you're the son of Jim and Mary Sheldon. I recall, that Jim was a real handyman. A blacksmith, right? You weren't home that night I had them for dinner. Well, kid, you'll be joining your folks soon enough."

He took a sluggish step toward me. Even though he was bloated from his huge meal, he was still ready to add me to the menu. I pulled the trigger on the Peacemaker and the bullet hit him right in the chest. All the time I'd spent shooting apples off the tops of fence posts finally paid off. Of course, he did provide a nice big target.

Stinking black blood gushed from the wound. He covered the ragged hole with his hand, but the clotted filth kept pouring out between his fingers.

"What the hell?" The vampire fell to the ground and tried to crawl toward me. But, with so much blood on the ground around him, he just flopped and wallowed like a dying pig in a muddy sty. "How is this possible? Bullets can't hurt me. They can't, they just *can't*..."

"Well, it looks like mine did," I said in my best matter-of-fact voice. "My bullets are made from a silver cross that belonged to my mother. I melted it down myself. My father *was* a blacksmith, like you said, and he taught me to work metal. The town priest told me your kind can't stand blessed silver. Glad to see he was right."

The vampire stared up at me. "No. I can't die!"

"Give it a try, mister."

Within a minute, his blood turned to pale gray ash, and so did his flesh and bones. I ran over and kicked the ashes and they went flying into the night sky, tossed higher and higher by the wind.

A SWIM IN THE MOONLIGHT

by Mark McLaughlin

You there, boy! On the bike. Come over here.

Going to see the Theodorakis sisters, are you? And what do you have there? A rose? And a present, perhaps, in that tote bag?

Which lucky sister will receive your rose—Thalio or Erato? Or haven't you made up your mind yet? Both are very beautiful. Different, but—

Thalia? The plump one, is it! It's amusing, how skinny boys like you always fall for her.

Hold it, my friend! I'm not done talking to you. My name is Spiro and I'm enjoying a bit of anisette. Care to join me? There's some left in the bottle. Why don't you finish it off? If Thalia isn't expecting you right away, perhaps we can chat for a while. There are a few things about the Theodorakis sisters I think you should know.

Sit with me here on the porch. I've been neighbors with the ladies for fifteen years.. They're a bit older than one might think.

You like older women? I should say! Still, they look the same today as when I first laid eyes on them. Erato with her thick black hair and long legs. So slender. And then there's Thalia with her fine curves, like wonderful scoops of vanilla ice cream. Eyes a big and green as a jungle cat's. I look at the sisters and sometimes I forget—

Finished with the bottle so soon? Such a boy! Just like my friend Nick. Ah, poor Nick. He used to share this house with me. Drank like a fish, he did. But funny! Just a look from him could make me laugh. We used to work together at my father's store. One day Nick showed up with booze on his breath and Papa kicked him right out the door.

Papa never understood my I let Nick stay with me. But what was I going to do—let my best friend turn into a bum? You had to love him! Once, when he'd had too much to drink on Thanksgiving, he walked down this very street with a turkey neck hanging out of his pants. Did a little dance, too. An old woman in a car yelled at him and he threw the turkey neck at her. She swerved right off the road!

Too bad Nick's not alive today. He could have made good money as a comedian. These days, every comedian has his own TV show. As it was, Nick made a buck here and there. Odd jobs. You know, you look a bit like Nick. What do *you* do, boy?

I'm not familiar with that line of work. What exactly is a performance artist…?

Oh…. Sounds interesting! Very creative. Perhaps Nick could have been a performance artist.

I remember the day the Theodorakis sisters first stopped by. It was about a week after they'd moved into the house down the road. They invited us to take a dip with them in their pool. Nick would have jumped in fully dressed if it wasn't for me. He knew I was afraid of water.

Why? Oh, it goes back to my childhood—doesn't everything? Papa tried to teach me how to swim by throwing me in the river. I almost drowned! And yet the next week he did it again. My father was a stubborn man. All he managed to do was to give me bad dreams. Nightmares about a giant squid pulling me under the waves, tearing at me with its horrid beak. What dreams those were! So much for Papa's swimming lessons.

Instead of swimming, the four of us had a picnic. It was like a dream, my friend—two beautiful Greek women, just down the street! Rich, too. Surely you've seen their gold rings. Erato told me that Spiro was a wonderful, manly name. Thalia said she liked Nick because he was funny and American.

Every night, we went bowling, saw movies, ate in restaurants, you name it. At first Papa was upset when he found out I was spending so much money on a girl. But when I told him she was *Greek,* he lined my pockets with cash! He even threw in a few bucks for Nick, to make amends. Papa's died a few years back—I never told him what I'll soon be telling you about the sisters.

Thalia and Erato picked their house because it had a pool. The two of them were always talking about how much they liked to swim at night. Erato would say to me, "Spiro! A big strong man like you, afraid of the water! Wouldn't you like to swim with me in the moonlight?"

After a while, I decided to take a dip—so long as I could wear an inner tube around my middle. What can I say? Old fears die hard. Of course, Erato was delighted. At that time, I would have done anything for her.

It was Friday night…the night we were to have our pool party. Nick was working for a printer at the time. He came home and showered…he reeked of that awful ink…and we went to buy champagne and some gifts for the sisters.

While we were shopping, Nick asked if there was a Muse for printing. Of course, the answer was easy: No! The ancient Greeks didn't have printing presses. He was always coming up with crazy mythology questions. As if I should know all the answers because I'm Greek. Nick was funny, but smart? Not so much.

I do know quite a few of the old legends, though. Once we started talking about the Muses, Nick asked me to name them all. I had to give this some thought: there was Clio, the Muse of history…. Terpsichore, the Muse of dance….

Then I remembered—Thalia and Erato were the names of Muses. Thalia was the Muse of comedy and Erato was the Muse of love poetry. How delightful, I thought: we each had our own goddess!

At the pool, I joked with the sisters. I asked how Zeus was, and is Aphrodite and Circe would be stopping by later. Not so very funny—not like Nick. But Thalia and Erato laughed like crazy women. They laughed and laughed until they were hoarse. It was strange … their laughter reminded me of dogs barking.

Finally I got into my inner tube and Nick helped me into the water. You probably think nothing of a fine swim. Me? I had a hand on the pool ladder but still, my stomach felt full of worms. I was brave, though, for my Muse.

As the Theodorakis sisters slipped into the water, Nick tried to hand me a champagne bottle, but lost his balance and fell in the water. I was so startled, I let go of the ladder. How pitiful we were!

Suddenly something grabbed me by the foot. I was so shocked that I soiled my swim trunks. It was like my nightmare—something cold and slimy was pulling me down into the water. But it wasn't a squid.

Do you know any of the old stories, boy? Perhaps you learned some Greek mythology in college, yes?

The moon was very bright. I could see Erato beneath me in the pool. Her neck was now wreathed with blood-red gills. How many times I had kissed that neck! Her hands were covered with fish scales. Her long, slender legs had … changed. Changed into dozens of squirming tentacles. But that wasn't the worst of it. Each tentacles was tipped with a small head—like a rat's, my friend, except that rats do not have thick lips and huge jutting eye-teeth.

One of those tentacles was wrapped around my ankle. Its horrid, fanged head bit deep into my leg. I could feel that monstrous mouth sucking at me, trying to drink the life out of me. Soon the water around me was clouded with blood, hiding Erato from sight.

Nick tried to help me, but then the water seemed to carry him to the other end of the pool. But it wasn't the water—it was Thalia. She was huge now, a swollen shadow just beneath the surface. Her green eyes waved about on the ends of fleshy stalks. Foam whirled and churned through the cavern of her mouth. A grey claw reached up and pushed Nick into that cavern—teeth like knitting needles sank into his flesh….

Suddenly I saw the champagne bottle bobbing in the water. I grabbed it and broke it against the ladder, then stabbed down into the water with it, slicing both the tentacle and my leg. In a moment, I was able to twist free. I grabbed the ladder and pulled myself to safety. Erato joined her sister—and Nick—at the other end of the pool.

* * * *

Muses? Perhaps by day, on dry land.

The Theodorakis sisters are unaware of their dual existence. The next morning, they found me unconscious on the lawn and took me to the hospital. They had no idea what happened to Nick. Erato did mention that she'd seen a broken bottle in the pool. They figured the blood in the water was from my slashed leg.

Some of the blood, yes. But not all of it.

I have no idea what happened to Nick's body. Did they eat it or just suck out all the blood, like vampires? If anything was left, did they hide it? Who knows!

Since then, they have lured many young men to their deaths. And until now, I have not intervened. After all, Thalia and Erato are sur-vivors of the ancient world, I'm sure. Who am I to mess with their affairs?

But you, my friend … you are the image of Nick.

Your college courses…. Do you recall the legend of Jason and the Argonauts? An adventure filled with strange perils—and monsters. While sailing to Crete with the Golden Fleece, Jason and his men encountered—

Very good, but you mispronounced both names. Repeat after me: Scylla and Charybdis.

Now tell me, what's in that tote bag? Show me….

Ah! Swim trunks, a towel!

On your way to a pool party? A little swim in the moonlight…?

IN THE GUTTER

by Mark McLaughlin

A lean, red-haired attendant entered the waiting room from the clinic's inner offices. "We're ready for you, Mr. Zugman," she said. "Right this way."

Gripping the mildewed arm of the couch, Zugman attempted to push his flabby bulk up from the seat cushions. The receptionist, a thin blonde with a dark-orange faux tan, rolled her eyes and sighed. Finally, she left her dental metal desk to assist, lifting him under his elbow. The attendant helped, too, until at least they brought Mr. Zugman to his feet.

"Thank you, ladies," he wheezed. He smiled feebly. "I could have used your help getting out of bed this morning." The two women exchanged a look which made the big man feel small indeed.

The attendant retreated into the clinic and Zugman lumbered after her. They advanced down a hall lined with windows on one side and numbered pine doors on the other. Zugman glanced out the nearest window. In the street below, an elderly drunk pissed his name— *Ted*—into a snowbank.

The attendant ushered Zugman through door No. 7 into a small room with an examination table, a chair, a full-length mirror and a sink with a counter. "Miss Edna will be with you shortly," the attendant said. "Please take the green pills in the cup by the sink."

He found the pills and did as he was told. "I can hardly wait," he said. "I've always been fat, you know. Always."

The lean woman nodded. "Miss Edna will take care of you. Now remove your clothes." With a curt nod, she left the room, slamming the door shut.

Zugman draped his topcoat and silk suit jacket over the chair. After a moment's hesitation, he pulled off the rest of his clothes and folded them into a large, neat bundle.

Naked, he studied his reflection in the full-length mirror. God, but he was a wreck—a mass of flab and stretchmarks. His bellyflesh was rutted from botched liposuction sessions. Scars from various surgeries criss-crossed his abdomen. His wrists were scarred, too. In layers.

The door opened and Zugman put his hands over his groin. even though rolls of hid his genitalia.

Miss Edna moved into the room. She was a bony, pale woman with dark hair and a long nose. She wore a loose yellow dress, many sizes too large for her, as well as sandals and a jarring accessory: grey suede gloves. She closed and locked the door behind her.

"My, my, my," she said, pinching Zugman's forearm, chest and rear in rapid succession. "I may have to charge you for overtime."

The fat man raised an eyebrow. "You *are* joking."

"Of course, of course," Edna said with a chuckle. "I take it you have my payment…?"

"Five-thousand dollars—and worth every cent, if this works. I've always been fat, you know. As big as a house."

"Yes, I'm sure." The pale woman nodded impatiently. "So how is our friend, Mrs. Kingston?"

"Aggie is fine, thank you. She looks positively marvelous." He found himself staring at the suede gloves. "You do excellent work."

Zugman was Agatha Kingston's divorce lawyer. The rich and newly thin socialite had given him the clinic's private number. This session was the culmination of many truly astounding consultations.

"A pity you have to keep your clinic out of the public eye," he said. "Here in the gutter." The pills were making him feel lightheaded. His skin felt hot and thick, like sun-warmed mud.

As the pale woman pulled off her gloves, a riot of clicks and squeals filled the room. Unleashed, her slender fingers stretched into fleshy prehensile tubes, each ending in a gnashing beak.

"The poor babies are ravenous. You're my first client of the day." So saying, Miss Edna stepped forward and plunged her fingers into his sagging belly. He could feel the eager tubes racing under his skin, sucking up fat.

Delightful.

As her horrific fingers sucked down more and more fat, Miss Edna's hips and thighs swelled under her loose dress. Soon her stomach and upper arms expanded as well. The process had been explained in detail to Zugman: this session was little more than a snack to Miss

Edna and her voracious hands. If he had any chubby, discreet friends, he was encouraged to share the clinic's private number with them.

He moaned with pleasure as Miss Edna slid her fingers deeper. *Deeper*. At last, he would be free. Free of his abhorred fat.

* * * *

Several months later, Zugman confronted Miss Edna outside of the clinic after work.

The pale woman had been busy that day. Her hips and thighs were laden with fat deposits. Of course, with her active metabolism, she would have that blubbery bounty depleted within days.

"You've got to do me again," Zugman said, grabbing her by the arm.

"Why? You're as thin as a reed." She pulled free and back toward the clinic.

"Don't mock me!" Zugman stared at her with bloodshot eyes. "I've always been fat. As big as a house! A whale! Can't you see?" He ran his hands over his lanky frame. "Nothing has changed. You've got to help me!"

"I was afraid this might happen." Miss Edna spoke with cold authority. "I had my doubts about your psychological profile. I only took on your case because of your association with Mrs. Kingston. I think perhaps your problem requires the services of … another sort of professional."

"You cheated me, you filthy bitch!" the haggard man cried.

Miss Edna gasped. "You cannot talk to me that way."

"Bitch. Slut. Freak." Zugman laughed hoarsely.

"I provide a needed service. I help people." The pale woman's eyes narrowed. "I must ask you to apologize."

"Apologize? To a fat-sucking harpy? To a monster?" He moved closer, sneering. "I paid good money and I'm not leaving without seeing some results. We're here in the gutter, bitch—so what the hell. *Gut me!*"

Miss Edna opened the clinic door and stepped inside. Her hands began to twitch hungrily. Uncontrollably.

"Right this way, Mr. Zugman," she whispered.

DRACULA HAS RISEN FROM THE SOFA

by Mark McLaughlin and Michael McCarty

Morgulla, the oldest of Dracula's three undead wives, pursed her luscious crimson lips as she threw a sofa pillow at him. She was a stocky blonde with bangs that nearly covered her deep-set violet eyes. "Get up already, you bloated human tick!" she cried. "We should never have had cable installed. All you do is watch that stupid flat-screen TV, night after night after night of the living dead."

Dracula replied with a hearty belch, flinging the drained carcass of yet another elderly man into the blazing fireplace. "Blah blah blah! Go down to that retirement complex and get me another victim. And pick one out with some meat on his bones. That last one was too scrawny." The rotund Count then grabbed the remote and searched the channels until he found a rerun of The Sunset Girls, a program about four plucky, elderly women sharing a ranch-style house. "Hey, this is my favorite show!"

"Ha! Every show is your favorite show," Morgulla said.

"No, really. Look at those silver foxes! Daddy likes!" Dracula rubbed his puffy, pale hands together. "They may be old bats, but they're still younger than you three! Now hurry down to that retirement complex—and get me a woman this time. Find one who looks like that tall broad on TV—what a hottie! Maybe we should find a place like theirs. No stairs! This old castle has way too many grand stairways!"

"When was the last time you climbed even a single step?" said Nausma, the next oldest of his wives. She was pale and thin with an elaborately curled auburn coiffure nestled atop her round, wide-eyed head. "I can't remember the last time you left that sofa. And anyway, that retirement complex is practically empty now. The only ones left are on life-support. They'd be dead before we got them to you. And before you ask: the village is out of babies. And so is every village within a fifty-mile radius." She pointed to the crackling fireplace. "Why'd you have to guzzle Mr. Tillman's blood all at once? He could have lasted you two or three nights."

Dracula waved a long-taloned hand dismissively. "A dog then. A Rottweiler or some overweight hunting dog sounds yummy right now. Bring me a fat, lazy dog!"

Nausma crossed her arms. "I don't have to. I'm looking at a flabby old bloodhound right now. You eat all the servants and never help with the housework! Look at all the filthy curtains in this room—they haven't been cleaned in more than a century! All that black velvet is filled with dust, cobwebs, and dead bugs. Disgusting!"

Verma, the youngest of the vampire's spouses—she'd recently celebrated her two-hundred and thirty-second birthday—marched up to her husband and stamped her dainty foot. She was a slender, birdlike creature with lank raven hair and a hooked nose. "I used to be a princess of Vultravia. I had it all going on. I could have been queen, for Anti-Christ's sake. But no, I had to give it up to be one of your brides. And for what, I ask? So I can listen to you and those two ancient harpies argue for hours on end?" She turned to the other wives. "No offense."

"None taken," said Morgulla.

"Hell, I'm the first to admit I'm a harpy," Nausma stated.

"Pipe down, you filthy crones," Dracula hissed. "I'm trying to watch the show!"

"Oh, this is too much!" Morgulla cried. "You pompous, flatulent bag of buzzard guts! You have a bunch of perfectly good dead chicks at their respective sexual peaks, standing right here in front of you— but you'd rather waste your time gawking at the living on that idiot box! Utterly ridiculous!"

"I think we should tell him!" Verma said.

Dracula looked up at the youngest bride. "Tell me what?"

His three wives said nothing, but shot quick, guilty glances at each other.

Enraged, the Dark Lord turned off the television. "Well? Tell me what?"

"If you must know…" Verma turned away from him. "We're seeing another monster."

Dracula broke the remote control in half. "What!" Suddenly he realized what he'd done to the device. "Oh, crap!" he whimpered, staring at the shards of broken plastic and circuitry in his hands. "Look what you made me do!"

Morgulla stifled a laugh.

The Count grabbed another remote from a cherrywood end-table next to the sofa. "And that was my favorite remote too! Now I have to use my back-up remote!"

Now all three of the brides were laughing.

"So who is this fancy-schmancy monster you three are seeing? It's not that Frankenstein's Monster, is it?" The King of the Vampires gnashed his fangs with fury. "That bastard is a complete phony—and a complete mimbo. You know what a 'mimbo' is? A male bimbo! You don't know where his parts have been!"

"No, it's not Frankenstein's Monster," said Morgulla, "though rumor has it that he's quite the love machine! I hear he's got a case of trouser rigor mortis that just won't quit. If only we had that same problem with you!"

"It's not that Wolfman freak, is it?" Dracula countered. "He does it with dogs, you know. Doggy-style with actual dogs! Is that the kind of kinky canine creep who turns you on?"

"I wouldn't mind it if that dog threw me a bone!" Nausma said. "But no, it's not the Wolfman."

"Good! I don't want any of you bringing his fleas home." The vampire thought for a moment. "Oh no…. It's not the Gill-Man, is it? Don't tell me it's that web-fingered, stinky-assed, chum-for-brains Gill-Man!"

Verma rolled her eyes. "I think you'd know if any of us were having an affair with the Gill-Man. I mean, we'd be coming home all wet and streaked with seaweed—and of course, vampires have to stay away from running water. He's not exactly what we'd call a love connection."

Dracula nodded. "Yeah, I should have known it wasn't the Gill-Man. None of you are that desperate." Suddenly he glared at his wives, his eyes glowing neon-red with diabolical fury. "Don't tell me it was the Mummy—I hate that dirty, dehydrated son of a jackal!"

Verma rolled her eyes. "Puh-leeeeze! There might be some petri-fied wood under all those bandages, but he's just too dependent on his mother, the queen of Egypt. Nobody wants a mummy wrapped up in his mommy!"

Dracula shook his head, like a groggy drunk starting to sober up. "What am I doing? Why am I even playing this ridiculous guessing game? I'm the master of this castle of dread—and under this roof, my undead word is law! I demand you tell me who is schtupping my unholy brides!"

At that moment, something stirred in a far corner of the room. A dark, thin object, about a foot long, hovered in the shadows—then it rushed across the room, straight toward Dracula. Strangely enough, the projectile seemed to be making a sort of odd flip-flopping sound, like bare feet running across a room.

The projectile soon found its target. Amazed, the vampire rose from the sofa. He looked down at his bleeding chest and gasped.

A wooden stake had been driven into his heart.

"But how—? Who—?" Suddenly the answer dawned on him. "The Invisible Man!"

"At your service. Funeral service, that is!" chuckled a deep, self-satisfied voice, seemingly from out of nowhere. "Quicker than the eye, you're gonna die!" said the Invisible Man with a gravelly laugh.

Dracula moaned, trembled, then collapsed to the floor as a pile of grainy, blue-gray particles.

Morgulla went to the closet, pulled out a vacuum cleaner and used it to suck up the dark mound of dust. Nausma noticed that the blaze had died down in the fireplace, so she threw in some logs to get it roaring again. After Morgulla had finished vacuuming, Verma ran a damp sponge over the floor and sprayed the sofa with disinfectant.

The Invisible Man threw open the windows. "Let's get some fresh air in here. This whole place stinks of sweat and rotten meat."

Nausma picked up the wooden stake. "Nothing easier than a good old-fashioned Transylvanian divorce! No paperwork! No lawyers!" She flung the weapon into the flames. "And the wives get the house!"

Morgulla tossed the vacuum cleaner bag into the fire. A moment later the bag exploded, filling the fireplace with swirling flames and dark green smoke. "There! Good riddance to bad rubbish!"

Verma examined the sofa cushions. "Now, did we get rid of every little piece of him? He's pretty tricky. He can regenerate from even the weensiest little fleck of dandruff, you know."

"Oh, quit your worrying. He's gone, and that's that!" the Invisible Man said. "Ladies, it's time to check out the master bedroom!"

Giggling with delight, the merry widows ran up the stairs to the boudoir, followed by their randy transparent lover.

A moment later, a little brown mouse crept out a hole in the wall. The ravenous rodent scurried around the room, looking for something to nibble on. Next to the sofa, lodged in a crack in the floor, he found a tiny sliver of toenail.

An evil toenail.

The mouse sniffed at it, trying to figure out what it was. Finally the beast gnawed off a bit of the nail and swallowed it. With a squeak of agony, the mouse fell to the floor, writhing.

A minute later, he rose up on his hindlegs. His beady little eyes glowed blood-red. His hairy lips parted, revealing jutting, needle-sharp fangs. Then hairy, membranous wings popped out of his back, and the mouse became a vampire bat.

With a shriek of triumph, the ungodly creature spread his hellish wings, flew over to the big-screen TV, and pressed the ON button with his snout.

As *The Sunset Girls* returned to the screen, the bat settled on a couch cushion and watched the show with rapt attention. When the credits began to roll, the bat rose into the air and began flying in circles, faster and faster. The circling bat soon dissipated into a swirling cloud of dark green mist, which settled back onto the couch and solidified into the rotund form of Dracula, tuxedo and all.

Dracula walked to the base of the stairway and listened. He could hear his three wives moaning with ecstasy as the Invisible Man pleasured them.

"All three of those rancid hags at the same time?" Dracula whispered. "Not only does that invisible gigolo have incredible stamina, but a strong stomach to boot! I can barely stand to look at all three at the same time!"

A few minutes later, the moaning stopped and Dracula heard the flip-flop of bare feet moving down the upstairs hall. Then the sound stopped.

"I'll be back!" the Invisible Man called out to his undead lovers. "I'm just going down to the wine cellar to see if there's any champagne!"

"That invisible bastard wants to drink all my hooch, too?!" Dracula whispered. Then the flip-flopping of the footsteps resumed, so the vampire hid in the shadows under the stairway.

The flip-flopping sound came down the stairs. When the sound reached floor level, Dracula rushed out of the shadows. Figuring the Invisible Man to be about six feet tall, he began slashing at the air with his talons in the general direction of his rival's neck.

"Aaaargh!" cried the Invisible Man. "You just scratched out my eyes! You fight like a girl!"

"Sorry! You're shorter than I'd thought!" Dracula said. Feeling around in the direction of the voice, he soon found the Invisible Man's throat and quickly sank his teeth into it. When he was finished, the vampire picked up his unconscious victim and threw him into the blazing fireplace.

"You were more than enough trouble as an invisible mortal," Dracula said. "I'm not going to risk having you come back as an invisible vampire!"

Ten minutes later, Morgulla, Nausma and Verma all came downstairs, garbed in black-lace nightgowns. The undead brides all looked happily exhausted from their bedroom gymnastics with the Invisible Man.

"He should have found the champagne by now…" Morgulla said.

"Oh, you know how men are!" Nausma cried. "They get lost so easily, and they hate asking for directions. Hey, do you smell something cooking?"

"Hey, look!" Verma said. "The TV is on."

Dracula looked up over the top of the couch. "I'm watching *Hex & The City*. If you're looking for your invisible playmate, you'll find what's left of him roasting in the fireplace."

"You killed the Invisible Man!" shrieked Verma.

"Hey, he killed me first!" the master vampire replied.

"Well, you've got a point there," Morgulla said. "But what a loss! He was so good in bed!"

"He's still hot stuff…" Dracula murmured with a smile, glancing at the crackling chunks in the fireplace.

"Well, you've had your revenge," Nausma said. "So I guess things will just go back to the way they were."

"Don't be too sure about that!" Dracula said, grabbing the backup remote control. He pushed a button and metal panels shot up around the vampire. The tops of the panels folded in and met above the sofa, encasing Dracula in a massive steel sarcophagus.

Inside the sarcophagus, a control panel sprang up from under the couch cushions. The Count pulled a large red lever at the top of the panel.

In the living room, hidden gears began to turn, drawing open the dusty velvet curtains. Morning sunlight poured through the windows, bathing Morgulla, Nausma and Verma in lethal radiance.

"Gotta love a Transylvanian divorce!" Dracula shouted inside the sarcophagus as his adulterous brides dissolved into blue-gray particles. "No court dates! No alimony! And the husband gets the house!"

DRACULA TRANSFORMED

by Mark McLaughlin & Michael McCarty

PROLOGUE

Burnt Bone

Professor LaGungo's Exotic Artifacts & Assorted Mystic Collectibles Tuttlesburg, Wisconsin

A burnt, broken finger bone…

Melina Papademetriou gazed through the dust-streaked glass of the display glass at the scorched relic. Yes, that's exactly what it was. A horribly abused human finger bone, resting on a purple plush pillow.

The shop, Professor LaGungo's Exotic Artifacts & Assorted Mystic Collectibles, featured thousands of bizarre curios, all set on a cluttered multitude of shelves and cherrywood tables. Not all of the merchandise was small: some items were quite large, like a pool table with a playing surface covered with a disturbingly pink hide.

Melina looked up at the shopkeeper. "That bone … can I take a closer look?"

Professor Artemis Theodore LaGungo gave the customer his warmest smile—which wasn't easy, since he was extremely old and his smile had grown increasingly chilly with the passage of time. "That's a rather pricey item," he said. "The fifth most expensive treasure in the store. I rarely remove it from the case."

Melina raised a slender black eyebrow. She was a dark-haired, thin-faced woman with full red lips and eyes as green as limes. She wore a long black trench coat, belted so tightly that only the green silk collar of the outfit beneath could be seen. "I have money."

"Of course you do," the Professor said. "But I can't imagine that such an item is something you'd want to buy." He turned and waved a gnarled, liver-spotted hand at the bizarre curios on the shop's many rows of shelves. "So many wonderful items from all over the world. Banned books, ancient relics, sacred skulls, amulets and so much more. I've spent a lifetime collecting them. I love them all—but, I do have to make the occasional sale. Business is business."

"How much does the bone cost?" Melina tapped the glass. "I have a strong feeling about it… An aura of tremendous power surrounds it." She held out her hand. "I just realized, I haven't introduced myself. My name is Melina Papademetriou."

The Professor gave Melina's hand a gentle shake. "I'm Professor LaGungo—of course, you saw my name on the door of the shop."

"Oh, I know who you are," Melina said. "I attended one of your lectures a few years back. The one about the Cult of the Internet Witches. Quite entertaining, and enlightening, too. Do you have any more lectures coming up?"

"Oh no, they take too much out of me," the shopkeeper said, pushing his thick glasses up the ridge of his nose with a bony finger. "Too much time, too much energy. Plus, they require me to leave the shop, and the place can't make money when the doors are locked. But I do thank you for saying the lecture was 'entertaining'—I've always tried to keep my presentations lively." He pointed down through the glass counter of the display case. "But, back to the bone: you mentioned that it radiates an aura. I take it you can see this aura?"

"Certainly." She gazed down at the relic, her bright green eyes wide with delight. "It radiates swirls of black, lead-gray and maroon. Not everyone can see these things." She looked up and stared into the Professor's eyes. "Whatever your price, I'll pay it. Money is not as issue." She took a large clutch purse from a coat pocket and opened it so the Professor could see the thick roll of bills inside.

The old man cradled his sagging jowls in his lean fingers. "Do you have any idea who once owned that gruesome little chunk of humanity?"

"Humanity…?" Melina shook her head. "I imagine its once-time owner wasn't all that humane. The aura tells a tale of great power and great evil. Clearly the owner had been a monster."

The Professor nodded. "That is true. So why do you want it so badly?"

"Do you really need to know?" Melina asked. "Are you worried that I'm going to do something awful?"

The Professor absentmindedly stroked a stuffed iguana resting on the counter. "Oh no, I'm not worried. Whatever you might do with the bone is your business. I'm simply curious, that's all! And perhaps you are curious, too. Would you like to know the identity of its past owner?"

The dark-haired woman nodded.

"Years ago," the Professor said, "I was traveling through southern Italy in search of a particular curio—the poisoned knitting needles of a lovely murderess who'd been married twelve times. Those golden needles had hastened most of her husbands to their final rest. Along the way, I stopped in a small village that was having some pest problems. Something was biting the citizens in the night."

Melina wrinkled her nose in disgust. "Rats? I can't stand rats."

"No, a vampire. Count Dracula, to be exact. Transylvanian sorcerer and nobleman, who claimed to be a descendant of Attila the Hun." The Professor opened the display case and brought out the pillow and its precious cargo. "I believe that was once the tip of one of his index fingers. He had been bothering the villagers for some time, until finally they hunted him down one night, forcing him to hide inside a farmer's well, clinging to the wall by his claws."

"May I hold it?" Melina said. She held out the clutch purse. "You can hang on to this, just so you can be sure I won't run out with the merchandise."

The Professor took the purse from her. "If you insist."

Melina's eyes narrowed to slits as she picked up the brittle treasure and examined it. "It's cold!"

"Is it really? I've never actually touched it with bare hands. Now where was I...?" The Professor stared into space for a moment, gathering his thoughts. "Oh yes: the vampire, trapped inside the well. A group of farmers poured kerosene over the Count and threw in a match. All this was happening the very night I arrived at the village, so I had the privilege of witnessing the proceedings firsthand."

"How exciting!" Melina placed the bone back on the pillow. She looked at her thumb and forefinger, rubbed them together, and looked again. "Interesting. My skin is all pale and wrinkled."

"I'm sure it'll be back to normal soon," the Professor said. "The bone drained a bit of life-force from you. But back to my story. The next morning, I visited the well and saw the end of that bone sticking out from between some stones in the wall of the well. It was all that was left of the Count—and fortunately, it was just within reach. I did have to borrow some pliers from a farmer to pull it out. It was really crammed in there."

Melina smiled. "You certainly were at the right place at the right time."

"I'm surprised you're not asking for any official documentation. That's an awful lot of money to spend on something you just noticed a few minutes ago."

"That aura is all the proof I need. And as for the amount: I have more money than I could ever hope to spend. I'm not going on welfare any time soon." She pointed to the purse. "Take out however much you like. I'm not one to haggle."

The Professor opened the purse, took out twenty-five thousand dollars, and then handed the purse back to his customer. "This will do fine, thank you. Consider it a fire sale."

The dark-haired woman laughed. "You are a marvelous fellow, Professor LaGungo. Thank you for the story and my new treasure. Do you have a box for it?"

"Certainly!" The Professor walked to a nearby shelf and picked up a small wooden box painted with zebra stripes. "On the house. The box has a story behind it, too, but I won't take up any more of your time."

* * * *

That evening, Melina carried the zebra-striped box down the thirty-six steps leading into the cellar of the main house of her estate. She hadn't lied to the Professor: she really *did* have more money than she could ever hope to spend.

Melina loved her cellar. It was always so cool, being well below ground level. Certainly it was much larger and more elegant than most cellars, with its snow-white marble countertops and floors. Plus, few other cellars featured a walk-in freezer and a black marble altar.

She set the box on the altar before entering the freezer. A few minutes later, she came out carrying the frozen body of a red-haired woman. She carried the body with great ease, even though it was about the same size as herself.

She laid the body on the altar. "Today's your lucky day, Mary." She opened a compartment in the side of the altar and took out a gold necklace, comprised of a round bas-relief medallion strung on a thick chain. The design on the face of the medallion depicted a serpent with nine heads.

"Look at the lovely present I have for you," Melina said, slipping the necklace onto the body. Then she picked up the zebra-striped box. "And look what else I have. It's not lovely, but it's just what the doctor ordered."

She leaned forward and whispered into the corpse's ear. "Just think, Mary. After all this time, you're finally going to be a mother."

CHAPTER ONE

Blood From A Stone

33 Years Later ….

Golden Manor Health & Rehabilitation Center
Red Banks, New Jersey

The handsome, red-haired man walked down the long, dim corridor. He wore a long white coat with a gold medallion pinned to the lapel. He glanced at a wall clock—almost midnight. He wondered if the halls of this nursing home were just as dim at noon. He walked past the security guard station.

"Hey! Wait up," said a heavyset man in a coffee-stained uniform. His office chair creaked as he lifted himself to his feet. "How did you get in here?"

The red-haired man turned, smiled pleasantly at the guard, but said nothing.

The guard frowned. "Do you work here?"

The man in white shrugged. "I do have work to do here this evening." He stared at the guard with brilliant green eyes. "You seem tired. You should take a nap. Don't mind me. I'm just running an errand."

The guard opened his mouth to say something, but all that emerged was a yawn.

"Sleep, my fat friend," the green-eyed man said with a laugh. "Sleep until dawn. No one will know."

With a weary nod, the guard settled back into his chair.

The man in white continued down the hall, listening to the gasps and snores and machine beeps coming from the various rooms. Old people. Worn out bodies, clinging to life. It seemed odd to him that most creatures grew feeble with age. Shouldn't they grow stronger? That seemed to make more sense.

He saw that he was approaching the nurses' station. All the white-clad women were standing around, chatting and drinking coffee. Some were smoking cigarettes. One was even smoking next to a sign that said THANK YOU FOR NOT SMOKING. Of course, this was a night shift—the hard and fast rules of the day departed with the setting sun.

"May I help you?" asked a plump, middle-aged blonde nurse. All the nurses were clearly surprised to see him—their eyes were wide with curiosity, and perhaps attraction, too. The smoker quickly put out her cigarette.

The red-haired man decided to have fun with them. "I am Dr. Xenos. I am here to see one of my patients, a dear old friend of mine. I must say, it dismays me to see the lot of you chatting—and smoking!—on company time. Surely you have work to do."

"Dr. Xenos?" The plump blonde glared at him. "Never heard of you."

The man in white smiled, opened his green eyes wide and stared, his eyes slowly scanning from one woman to the next. "Really? That surprises me. I'm actually somewhat of a celebrity. People all over the world are familiar with my work. Are you sure you haven't heard of me? Think about it…search your minds…in fact, I bet if you all went to sleep, you'd probably remember and have lovely dreams about me. Why don't you do that? Fall asleep. Lovely dreams. Lovely. Al¹ About. Me."

ared and stared, and the nurses began to yawn. One by one,
om sight behind the counter of the nurses' station. Soon
v petite snores, and some that were not so petite.
ht, ladies," the red-haired man whispered as he con-

tinued on his way.

He approached the last door on the left, opened it and entered the darkened room. The only light came from a few tiny red bulbs on various monitors. The man in white could see perfectly well in the dark, and he drew closer to the bed. The old man sleeping there wheezed fitfully.

"Wake up, Dr. Van Helsing," he whispered. "Can I call you Abraham, or even Abe, after all these years?"

"Hmmm?" the silver-haired, bearded man stirred, than opened his eyes. He put out a hand toward the nightstand and fumbled with the lamp until he managed to turn it on.

"Well. It's you," he said, staring up at his visitor. "I recognize that look in your eyes. The rest is different… You're young now. With red hair? Your people don't have red hair."

"I am not typical of my people," the visitor said. "I can be many things, as you well know. And these days, I can be more things than ever. I thought that would amuse you." He laughed as he tapped the tip of the old man's nose with a forefinger.

"The fact that you have a sense of humor," Van Helsing said, "is probably the most surprising fact I've ever learned about you. How can one who is so evil, who has killed so many over the centuries, be able to laugh?"

"Because I am a child again," the man in white said. "The world is my playpen and your sort are my toys. And my baby bottles."

The old man looked him up and down. "You are very thin now. And young. Or at least, the appearance of youth. Your face looks… elfin. Angular. Feline, actually. Yes, like the face of a cat. Or a snake…." He frowned. "I wish I knew all of your secrets. That would make me happy, to know how one man—if indeed you are a man— can be so many things."

"Well, Abraham," the visitor said, "you may never learn all of my secrets, but soon I shall know all of yours." He opened his eyes wide, his brilliant green eyes. He smiled down at the old man. "So tell me."

"Tell you what?" Van Helsing asked.

The visitor shrugged lazily.

"This is absurd," the old man cried. "Why should I tell you any-thing?" He pressed the nurse call button.

"That won't do you any good," the man in white said. "Your keepers are asleep at their posts. Now tell me."

"I have nothing to tell you!" Van Helsing opened a drawer of his nightstand and pulled out a Bible. "I take it you are still afraid of this?"

The red-haired man chuckled. "Sorry, no. Crosses, holy water, all that rubbish—the world's climate has changed, and I've changed with it." He snatched the book from the old man's hands and tossed it into the shadows beyond the foot of the bed. "Nobody believes in any of that garbage now, so why should I? I keep up with the times. There are so many exciting things to do these days. I love this new age of technology. It makes religion seem so…trite."

The visitor sat on the edge of the bed. "In a way, I'm practically a religious figure myself these days. People do feel compelled to share their woes—their confessions—with me. As though I were a priest." He stared at the old man. "So tell me what you want to tell. What you *need* to tell."

Van Helsing stared back. "This is foolishness. Some wicked game of yours." He looked into the red-haired man's brilliant eyes. "You are a beast. That's all you are. You remind me of a cat I used to have, back when I was little. A huge orange tomcat with a crook in his tail. He weighed over twenty pounds. He used to try to eat off my plate. That cat, he was always hungry. He would grab my cold cuts and run off with them. I used to love cold cuts lightly sprinkled with sugar. I wish I could have some right now, but I have diabetes."

"Really? Tell me more.…"

"Back then, I used to tease Nick Perkowski all the time," the old man said. "Once I made him eat a box elder bug, then he went off crying. I used to call him Crybaby Nick. Once I paid a seven-year-old girl to lift up her dress and show me her underwear. I was about nine years old then. I don't know why I did it—I suppose I was being naughty. But not *too* naughty: I knew the limits. When my mother died, my father changed from a loud, happy man to a quiet, sad man. I didn't cry at my mother's funeral. My mother was always so busy, she never talked to me very much, so I wasn't all that sad. But I felt bad that I wasn't as upset as my father. I should have been. I used to think there was something wrong with me that way.

"Every now and then I watched Nick's older sister Carla undress. I would climb up a tree outside their house at night and watch as she took off her clothes. Her underwear was very lacy and she had such creamy, beautiful skin. I was so stupid, I worried that watching her undress would make her pregnant. My parents never explained those things to me. My cat used to pee in my shoes. That cat—what was his name? I would kick the cat, and then feel bad that I did it, because he was only a stupid animal. A stupid animal who liked cold cuts, just like me. I cried when he was killed by the neighbor's dog. Tangerine, that was his name! Because he was orange and so tiny as a kitten. Who knew he would grow so big? I cried when that cat died, but I didn't cry over my mother. *Terrible.* I was a *terrible* child."

"More," the man in white whispered, staring intently. "More."

"My grandmother was put in a home, much worse than this one, and my father visited her every Sunday morning and I went with him, which meant I didn't have to go to church anymore. Back then I was happy about that, because I used to think church was very boring. Now it appalls me, to think that I used to hate church, the house of the Lord! In time Nick Perkowski became my best friend. His father had a pipe collection, and Nick stole one of the pipes and a leather pouch of tobacco and we used to sit in the toolshed behind his house and smoke that pipe until we both got sick and threw up. And once he stole a bottle of vodka and we did the same thing! Drank it down and then threw up! But we had fun doing it. When his father noticed that the vodka bottle was missing, he blamed Carla. She got the belt for that. We knew the truth, but we didn't say anything. *Terrible.*"

The man in white listened with a tight grin. His face seemed to glow with a faint inner light.

"But then I did something *very* bad," the old man said. "Nick never found out. I couldn't bring myself to tell him."

"More."

"No. I can't tell you anymore. It's too sad."

"More!" The red-haired man stroked Van Helsing's forehead, pushing back a wispy, silvery lock.

"I cannot! It was *terrible* of me, to…to…" The old man paused, then sighed heavily. "…to cheat on that essay. I don't know why I did it. I was at Nick's house—he had done his schoolwork, and I had for-gotten about the assignment. I saw his essay on his desk while he was out of the room, and that reminded me I hadn't written mine—and I didn't have enough time to do it. So I folded up his essay and stuck it in my pocket. Later, I went home and copied it all out, changing the wording to the way I would phrase things. Why did I do it? Poor Nick! He failed the class! He trusted me, but he was a fool to be my friend! I felt so bad—I assure you, after that, I never cheated again."

"Really?" the man in white said with a sly smile. "What about Anna?"

"You know about that, do you?" The old man began to cry. "I suppose you would. I'm sure you've done your research. Yes, I cheated on my dear wife. You want to hear about that, too? Is there some awful detail you don't know about yet?"

"I'm sure there is." He continued to run his hands softly, so softly, over the old man's forehead, then his neck and shoulders. "More, please."

"But why?"

"You don't want to know. More. *More.*"

"Please, don't make me tell you more," Van Helsing said. "My mouth is dry from all this talking."

The visitor sighed. "I'm not making you do anything."

"I met Anna in college. At that time I was studying astronomy, theology, the occult—nothing practical in the eyes of the business world, but I put all that I learned to good use. As well you know! My Anna—she had long, dark hair, brown eyes, full lips…fragile hands. She trusted me and gave me all the love she had in her heart. We were happy for many years. In time I became a teacher, and so we started talking about raising a family. Soon came the children, and I should have been happy. I had everything a man could want. Everything!

"But Anna had a sister. A plump girl, very plain. Big-boned. Yet she had a way of looking at a man that could drive him insane. Insane with lust. And she used to say such daring things. I was entranced by that woman. Why, I don't know."

"Delightful," the red-haired man whispered. His face glowed as brightly as a candle.

"No! It was terrible!" Van Helsing cried. "Every few nights, I would make some excuse, and then sneak off to rut with that foul whore. I couldn't help myself! It was like she had a spell over me. I don't know why I did it—and I don't know why I am telling you about it! Maybe you can tell me why I acted like such a pig. Why I hurt and dishonored my Anna, the only woman I ever loved."

"Because," the visitor said, "you are just a man. And men die. So men want to do all there is to do, before they reach the end."

"You devil. You are exactly right." The old man nodded sadly. "Anna found out about the affair and started seeing another man, clearly out of spite. It was someone she had met at church. *Church!* It hurt to realize that Anna could do that sort of thing—but I cannot blame her. I stopped seeing her sister, and Anna ended her relationship with that other man. We stayed together, but things were never the same.

"I tried to write a book…I never finished it. I drifted from job to job, city to city, trying to find reasons to spend as much time away from home as possible. Anna's mind began to deteriorate. I should have spent more time with her. I suppose I was looking for something to give my life meaning. And then—"

"Then?" The man in white leaned closer.

"Then I started hunting you."

"Ah." The visitor narrowed his eyes, and this made Van Helsing gasp.

"Are you going to kill me?" the old man said.

"You have more to tell me, I think. More."

"Do I? You know the rest. I chased you and kept chasing you. At times I've managed to stop you from destroying the lives of others. I've stopped you from turning entire cities into graveyards of the living dead. You've bitten me many times, but I've always managed to use to scientific methods to counteract the effects. Haven't turned into a vampire yet, you ghoul!"

"True," the red-haired man said with a smile, "but my bite has given you extraordinary longevity. You've aged quite slowly, and I must say, gracefully. Has no one ever questioned the fact that you are far older than any mortal has a right to be?"

Van Helsing shrugged. "It is very easy to change a date here, a date there, on paperwork. I've been my own son from time to time—I'm sure you've had to pull that trick yourself. But at last I will die, and for good, someday. But you—! Even after the stake has entered your heart—after your total destruction, time after time—somehow, you've always managed to return. Always. Why is that? *Why?* Tell me that! Tell me!"

The visitor laughed. He ran his hands along the old man's arms, over his belly and down his legs. He moved to the end of the bed and sat on a far corner. "Eeny meeny minny moe," he sang. "Catch Van Helsing by the toe." So saying, he grabbed the old man by the big toe of his right foot. "You want to know all my secrets. That, my friend, is never going to happen. But I will tell you this much. Tonight I shall reveal a power you've never seen before."

"Let go of me! How dare…" Van Helsing's words suddenly began to slur. He tried to sit up, but only fell back on the bed. "My skin…something is wrong with my skin…what have you done?" He seemed to have difficulty even blinking. His eyes refused to shut all the way. "Are you going to…drink my blood?"

"Me? Drink your bitter old blood?" The man in white shook his head with disgust. "No, thank you. I can nourish myself in many ways. Tonight, Abraham, I've come to you brimming with the powers of the gorgon. An ancient creature, but new to this modern era. And a gorgon does not drink blood. It is a sin-eater. It is a beautiful beast that feasts on the ugliness of the human soul. On lies. Deceit. Guilt. You have fed me well this evening. And those who have fed the gorgon must turn to stone. That is the way of things."

The red-haired man giggled as he beat his palms against Van Helsing's belly, which had hardened to the stiffness of leather. The sound reminded him of a kettledrum. His happy face was shining like a full October moon. His laughter was a roar of delicious thunder. Soon the old man's belly grew too hard to slap.

"Stone, my friend!" the monster cried. "That should ease your mind. You've never wanted me to sip your cherished Van Helsing essence, and I can't drink blood from a stone. Very soon you won't be able to feel anything. You'll like that. It will be peaceful."

The visitor walked back to the entrance. His shining face dimmed with each step he took away from the bed. The glow was gone by the time he opened the door.

He turned back to the bed. "You can be your own monument now," he said. "It would be silly to bury a rock." It then occurred to him that he was talking to a dead man, which was silly, too.

He stared at the stone man. It would be a mistake to leave such a disturbing curio behind.

He returned to the bed. He still had more work to do….

Twenty minutes later, he walked past the sleeping nurses, past the sleeping guard, out of the building and back into the night.

He was already at home.

CHAPTER TWO

Party Monster

The Residence of Mina Murray
Elmhurst, Illinois

"I never drink wine," said the red-haired man to the bartender. "Except for champagne, of course. Who can say 'no' to champagne?" The heavyset, bald man behind the bar handed him a flute of bubbly.

The red-haired man downed the glass in three swallows. "Another, please. I have an insatiable thirst this evening."

The Victorian-style home was jam-packed with friends, family, coworkers and neighbors, all gathered to celebrate the engagement of Jonathan Harker and Mina Murray. The red-haired man had slipped in with a group of laughing friends. He wore a pale-gray suit, a black turtleneck, and a golden medallion on a thin chain.

A tall, bearded man dressed in a navy-blue suit and bone-white cowboy hat stepped up to the bar. In one hand he held a recently emptied glass—in the other, an unlit cigar.

"Hello, Quincey P. Morris," said the red-haired man, holding out his hand.

Quincey turned to look at him. He put his cigar in his pocket so he could shake hands. He looked the fellow quickly up and down. "Do I know you, sir? You seem to know me. But I can't seem to recall your name—or face, for that matter. Generally, I'm good at sniffing out people's identities, like a coon-hound hunting down a critter in the night."

"I am Dr. Xenos. So you consider me to be a night-critter…?"

"Maybe so! Your hand is colder than a January night in Canada. You need to get more booze in your system to warm you up." The young Texan scratched his beard. "Dr. Xenos… Still doesn't ring a bell. What kind of doctor are you? Physician?"

"No, a psychologist."

"Oh…" Quincey said. "You must work with Sea Weed—I mean, Dr. Seward. I just like to call him Sea Weed."

"I do know Dr. Seward. He has a practice in St. Louis."

The Texan took his unlit cigar out of his pocket and held it in his hand. "I'm afraid I'm just a creature of habit," he said. "I always smoke when I drink. But the future Mr. and Mrs. Harker won't allow smoking in their house."

"No need to explain. I understand completely."

"Do you know Lucy Westenra? She has a thing for doctors."

"Does she? How delightful."

The Texan and his new friend crossed the room to the fireplace. Two young women stand in front of the fire—the flames gave their complexions a rosy glow. One was a statuesque blonde wearing a short black dress, while the other was a petite brunette wearing a white gown. The women turned toward Quincey and smiled.

"Lucy Westenra," Quincey said to the blonde, "I'd like to introduce you to Dr. Xenos."

"No first name?" Lucy said, holding out her hand to the red-haired man.

"It's Dax," he said, giving her hand a gentle squeeze. "A pleasure to meet you."

"And this is the woman of the hour, Mina Murray," Quincey said, nodding toward the brunette.

"Charmed," Dr. Xenos said, taking Mina's hand. "May your wedded life be filled with bliss."

"Thank you, doctor," Mina said. She turned to her tall friend. "That reminds me, Lucy. Don't forget, this Friday is the fitting for the dress."

"No worries, I'll be there," Lucy said. She flashed a mischievous grin at the doctor. "I love trying on dresses almost as much as taking them off."

Dr. Xenos laughed. "You're a wild one, I see!"

"Do you need a refill, Lucy? Doctor?" Mina asked.

They both said, "Yes," at the same time.

Mina took their glasses. "Escort me to the bar, Quincey. Let's give Lucy and the doctor a chance to chat."

As the Texan and the brunette walked off, Lucy turned to Dr. Xenos. "Alone, at last," she said. She dug into her purse and handed him her business card, which read *Lucy Westenra Escort Service.* He smiled as he tucked it into his pocket.

"Give me a call sometime," Lucy whispered. "For a freebie."

"You're too kind."

Quincey and Mina and returned with the drinks. Joining them was a dark-haired, thirtyish man with a moustache, and an older man with horn-rimmed glasses and salt-and-pepper hair.

"Dr. Xenos, this is my finance, Jonathan Harker," Mina said, nodding toward the thirtyish man. She then nodded toward the older man. "This is Dr. Seward."

"Good to meet you, Dr. Xenos," Dr. Seward said.

Quincey frowned. "I thought you two already knew each other." He turned to the red-haired man. "Isn't that what you said?"

Dr. Xenos nodded. "We *have* met before. But time was passed and I'm sure Dr. Seward meets new people all the time. So many faces, day in and day out."

"I have an excellent memory for faces," Dr. Seward. "I'd be inclined to think I'd remember you... Perhaps you've lost weight, or shaved off a beard?"

"I won't bore you with the details, but yes, my appearance has changed somewhat since last we met."

"Sorry, didn't mean to insinuate that you were lying!" Quincey said. He took a gulp of his Manhattan. "If I have too many of these, I won't remember *anybody's* face in the morning. So, now that we have Jonathan and Sea Weed, I guess the gang's all here!"

"Sort of," Jonathan said. "Dr. Van Helsing is too sick to attend. Last time I heard from him, he was in a nursing home. Arthur Holmwood is working on a new movie, and Renfield is still touring in England." Jonathan turned to Dr. Xenos. "Do you know Mina? Did she invite you...?" He glanced toward his fiancée, but she was deep in conversation with Lucy and wasn't paying attention.

"I've met Mina, yes," Dr. Xenos said. "You're a lucky man. She will make a lovely bride."

"Thank you," Jonathan said. "I wish I could stay longer to chat with everyone. But, it's already past my bedtime. I need to get up early tomorrow morning. I'm a pilot and I have a flight to Dallas."

"I must be moving along myself," the red-haired man said. "So many things to do this evening. I'm quite a night owl. I'm absolutely useless during the day."

Lucy looked up from her conversation with Mina. "Are you leaving, Dax honey? Talk with me for a minute before you go!"

As Dr. Xenos walked off with Lucy, Jonathan moved closer to Dr. Seward. "Aha! He's one of Lucy's clients," he whispered to his friend. "For a minute there, I thought he was some creep who'd slipped in while no one was looking!"

CHAPTER THREE

Autumn Storm

The Residence of Mina Murray
Elmhurst, Illinois

A week passed.

A damp, rainy evening fell upon Elmhurst. The wind whipped its chill across the prairie and plucked bright fragments of color from the trees, sending them spinning into the night's horizon.

In the attic of Mina Murray's house, the red-haired man pressed his face against the attic window as he watched the storm outside. The lightning cackled across the dark sky, illuminating the multi-colored leaves that soared through the air. A pair of bright headlights zoomed up the driveway. He hurried down the stairs, ran into her bedroom, and slid under the bed before she'd even opened the front door.

He had picked the lock and entered her house shortly after sunset. He'd spent some time with Lucy earlier in the week, and from her, had learned key information about Mina's schedule. He'd been able to spend a good ninety minutes going through every room of the house, examining her possessions.

He listened as she took off her raincoat, hearing the wet rustling of the rubberized fabric and the splash of raindrops on the hardwood floor. As the evening progressed, he smelled the leftover chicken noodle soup she heated up, and listened to the TV shows she watched as the hours melted into the night.

Bedtime neared, and he heard her gargle in the bathroom and brush her teeth. She entered the bedroom, and as she took off her clothes, he could hear her bra being unsnapped and her slacks being unzipped. He could even hear the gentle whisper of fine silk as she slipped on her nightgown.

Click: Mina turned off the light and crawled under her thick midnight-blue quilt.

The vampire slid out from his hiding place and sat on the edge of the bed.

"Good evening, Mina," he said. "A pleasure to see you again, Though I don't suppose you can see *me*."

"Who—? Dr. Xenos? Is that you?" Mina said, startled. "What's going on? Get the Hell out!"

"No, I am going to get *in*." He touched the side of her head. "Deep inside your brain."

She suddenly felt incredibly dizzy, like she was swirling down and down into an endless abyss. She fought to catch her breath.

"There's no need to fight me, dear," he said. "I am faster and stronger than you'll ever be. So *relax*. Close your eyes."

Mina did as she was told.

"Very good. Now, just follow the sound of my voice. We shall be going deeper and deeper and deeper into your mind."

"Deeper," she said in a soft, frightened voice.

"We are going to unlock the treasure chest where you keep all your secrets."

"Secrets," she repeated.

"There are plenty of secrets in there, I'm sure," he said.

"Yes. Lots and lots of secrets…" Her voice was still soft, but no longer frightened.

"I'm here to release them," the vampire whispered. "So let them go."

"I cheated on Jonathan."

"I see," he said with a smile. "Go on. With whom?"

"Quincey. Jonathan was away on business and Quincey wanted to fly me to Miami. But we didn't even make it out of the hangar."

"These things happen."

"When I was little, I kicked a puppy and it died," Mina said, tears streaming down her cheeks. "I didn't mean to kick it so hard. I think I was mad at my dad for … something. I can't remember what. Isn't that terrible? I killed a puppy and I can't even remember why I did it."

"Oh, you remember, Mina. Or rather, you *will* remember, if you just try harder. Now think. *Think.* What do you suppose your father might have done that would make you so very, very mad…?"

"I think…" Mina began to sob. "I think … Mommy wasn't home, and he'd been drinking and…." Her sobs grew louder and more anguished.

"Poor Mina," the red-haired man said. "Memories can be so hard to endure. But don't worry, soon you will be beyond the torment of such foul memories." He touched the golden medallion hanging around his neck. "By any chance, do you know the tale of the Lernaean Hydra?"

Still sobbing, Mina shook her head. "Noooo…."

"In Greek mythology," the vampire said, "the Hydra was a huge water-serpent with nine heads. Its lair was the sacred lake of Lerna. Beneath the waters of the lake was an entrance to the Underworld, guarded by the Hydra. For each head that any enemy might cut off, two more would grow back. The serpent was so vile, even its breath and blood were poisonous."

"What happened to the serpent?" Mina murmured. "Is it still alive? Is it going to kill me?"

"No, the serpent is not alive." He stroked Mina's tear-streaked cheeks. "Hercules killed the serpent as the second of his Twelve Labors. But yes, the serpent is going to kill you. The power of the serpent still survives. Through me."

So saying, he opened his jaws wide. If the lights had been on, Mina would have seen a mouthful of long, yellow fangs, dripping with pale green venom.

The vampire exhaled heavily. Swirling clouds of mist poured out of his mouth. The poisonous vapors rolled across the quilt and covered Mina's face. And because she had no way of knowing they were there, closing in on her—she breathed them in.

Her sobbing stopped as her eyes rolled back in her head. Her entire body began to shake violently, and watery froth began to pour from her lips, followed by vomit, and finally, gouts of blood.

"Poor little lamb," Dr. Xenos said. "I almost hated having to do that." He smiled in the darkness. "*Almost.*"

CHAPTER FOUR

Dark Star

Golden Manor Health & Rehabilitation Center
Red Banks, New Jersey

The black stretch limousine with the vanity license plate *Dark1* pulled into the nursing home's driveway.

When Ahmet, the chauffeur, opened the back door, out stepped a tall man wearing black jeans, a black silk shirt, black sunglasses, and a long black-leather jacket. His long black hair streamed out from under his black top hat. He carried a black walking stick topped with an ebony skull. The man's lips, nostrils and eyebrows were pierced, and his forehead featured a tattoo of a vampire bat.

Even at four in the afternoon, he was as scary as hell.

The dull stomp of the man's heavy black boots echoed down the poorly lit corridor. He stopped in front of the guard desk, where a heavyset man sat, checking his email on his cell phone. The name tag on his wrinkled brown uniform read *Stan Carlton: Head of Security*.

The visitor tapped his walking stick on the desk.

The guard looked up from his cell phone. It took him a moment to process the fact that he was in the presence of a celebrity. Finally he exclaimed, "Oh shit, you're Renfield! The Duke of Darkness! Dude, *Dead of Night* is my favorite CD of all time. I have all your CDs. Can you sign some? I have a few of them in my car."

Renfield cleared his throat. "I didn't fly over 3,500 miles, from England to New Jersey, just to chat with a fanboy. I have urgent business here. I am looking for one of your residents: Abraham Van Helsing."

A look of worry crossed the guard's face. "Are you a member of his immediate family?"

"Of course not," Renfield said. "He's a friend. I've known him for years. Grand old fellow."

The guard motioned for the Goth rock star to come closer. "He's no longer here. He *left*," he whispered. "I was working the night shift. The next day, he was no longer here."

"He checked out?"

"Not exactly. I checked the video from the security cameras and he never left his room. He had one visitor that night … some red-haired guy. We're not sure how he disappeared."

"Can I see the video?"

"I'd love to help you out," the guard said, "but if I get caught I'd get in a lot trouble. Maybe even fired."

Renfield reached into his pocket and pulled out five one hundred dollar bills. He placed the Benjamin Franklins on the counter. "We'll be discreet."

The guard quickly snatched up the cash. "Will you sign my CDs, too?"

"Of course."

* * * *

Stan the security guard and Renfield watched the video monitor. They saw the red-haired man come and go, but other than that, all they saw was a lot of empty hallway.

"Is there anything else you can tell me about Van Helsing's disappearance?" Renfield asked. "Could he have been carried out through the window?"

The security guard shook his head. "The windows are designed so they'll only open a few inches. Not enough for someone to crawl through."

"Hmmm…" Renfield thought for a moment. "Maybe the guy chopped up Van Helsing and slid the chunks out through the window. Is that possible?"

"Hell no! If that was the case, they'd be blood all over the place, and there sure wasn't any blood. Lots of dirt, but no blood."

Renfield's eyes grew wide. "*Dirt?* Tell me about that."

"It was really weird," Stan said. "I wasn't there, but according to the cleaning lady, the whole floor of the room was covered with white dirt. Broken rocks and gritty dirt. She had to vacuum for half an hour. She changed the bag five times! I'm the only person she's told about that—she's my girlfriend, Miranda—so I'd appreciate it if you kept that information to yourself."

"Why doesn't she want anyone else to know about the dirt?"

Stan took a swig of coffee from a mug with the words *World's Greatest Lover* on the side. "Administration wouldn't understand. They'd think she hadn't been doing her job. If they find a muddy footprint on the floor, they bitch at her for half an hour. Can you imagine how hard they'd have reamed her out if they'd found all that dirt in a patient's room? She'd have never heard the end of it."

"I see…." Renfield stood up. "Thank you for your time today, Stan. I appreciate it."

Stan stood as well. "You're welcome. I am confused, though. It seems like you knew something was going to happen to this Van Helsing guy."

Renfield nodded. "I did. I've been having strange dreams lately. Van Helsing used to tell me stories about an old enemy of his, and in those dreams, I see that enemy coming back to destroy Van Helsing, as well as the descendants of many of his friends. Over the years, I've learned to trust my dreams and act upon them immediately."

"Wow!" the security guard said. "Your private life is just as cool as your music!"

"It may be cool," Renfield said, 'but that old enemy is also after me."

"Bummer! I'm glad that guy ain't after me!" Stan flashed the rock star a huge, goofy grin. "I gotta say, it has been a total blast, hanging out with the Duke of Darkness. I sure hope that mean guy doesn't kill ya!"

* * * *

Back at the limousine, Ahmet opened the door for Renfield, who took his place in the back. He picked up his laptop from the floor and turned it on.

"How did it go, boss?" the driver asked, once he was behind the wheel again.

"Fine, Ahmet," he said. "Fine for me, anyway. Not so fine for Van Helsing. I think I've figured out who he'll go after next. Vampires always go after the prettiest and sweetest girls first…" He studied the screen of his laptop for a few minutes before typing in some information. "How far away is the Newark Liberty International Airport?"

"Thirty-seven miles, boss."

"Good, we'll get there in plenty of time." Several keystrokes later, he said. "I just booked us a flight to O'Hare."

CHAPTER FIVE

A Scream In The Night

The Residence of Lucy Westenra
Downers Grove, Illinois

Lucy stepped out of the shower and began to towel off. She'd endured a tiresome evening, having dinner with a particularly tedious client. The gentleman in question was eighty-seven years old, and while he didn't request any amorous favors, he did insist on telling her a string of lengthy anecdotes about his deceased wife Lorraine, poor Lorraine, who'd passed away ten years ago. Lorraine had died of lung cancer, but she'd also suffered from chronic fatigue syndrome, psoriasis, diabetes, sinus infections, and a sorry string of other ailments.

"When she was alive," the old guy had said, "I used to listen to her shuffling through the house, always coughing and sniffling and moaning, and I'm sorry to say, I would actually *pray* for her to die. But now that she's dead... Oh, how I miss her! What I wouldn't give to hear her shuffling through the house again. At least that would be better than silence. Night after night after night of silence."

Listening to the old guy's tales of medical misery had sapped her strength. But, she now felt revived after a nice hot shower.

She slipped on her fuzzy white robe and tied it shut with its equally fuzzy white belt. She wrapped a towel around her hair and opened the bathroom door. And there stood Dr. Xenos, grinning like Lewis Carroll's Cheshire Cat, ready to exchange witticisms with the befuddled blonde who fell down the rabbit hole.

"Good evening, Lucy," the vampire said. "A pleasure to see you again."

"Wha—? Dr. Xenos?" she cried, startled. "What are doing here? How did you get in?"

"A thousand apologies," he said with a devilish grin. He was wearing a black suit with a maroon turtleneck sweater. The medallion hung from a red leather cord. "I truly enjoyed meeting you at that wonderful party. I kept forgetting to schedule an appointment, so I thought I'd just stop by. As to how I found my way in: there was once a time when I could only gain entrance upon invitation. But I am happy to say, my current incarnation is not bound by that limitation. I've developed quite a knack for picking locks."

"Listen, Doc," she said, exasperated. "I appreciate your enthusiasm, but I don't like folks busting into my house, and half of that stuff you said sounded pretty creepy. Why don't you just leave the same way you came, before I call the cops?" The belt on her robe was starting to slip so she pulled it tight again. "Damn robe. It won't stay shut."

"Do you find me handsome, Lucy?" he said.

She nodded. "Sure. Handsome but crazy. You still have to leave."

"Are you sure?" he asked, holding out his hand. "I'm sure you are as forgiving as you are lovely. Surely you can forgive a handsome devil with an eye for beauty. Do you like my eyes?"

Lucy looked into his brilliant green eyes. "Sure…" she murmured. "They sure are green…like the green hills of Kentucky where I grew up."

"As green as a serpent's scales," Dr. Xenos said. "Or a serpent's eyes, for that matter. Green is such a soothing color, don't you think?" He stared into her eyes, pulling her very soul under his control. He held out his hand. "Let us go into the living room and have a chat."

She willingly put her hand in his. They walked through the house to the living room, where they sat on the couch.

Dr. Xenos looked deeply into Lucy's lustrous blue eyes. "I am going to probe your mind," he said. "Tonight I will get to know each other quite well. You are getting sleepy, aren't you, my dear?"

"Sleepy…" Lucy said softly. "Yes, so sleepy."

"Just listen to my voice. I want you to tell me everything you know about Quincey P. Morris."

"Quincey?" Lucy echoed, confused.

"Yes, your dear friend Quincey. I understand he is from Texas. Where exactly does he live?"

"He lives on a ranch in Blanco, Texas, near the Blanco River."

"I see."

"He lives on Ranch Road 165."

"Does his home have an alarm system?"

"No, I don't think so…." Lucy thought for a moment. "But he does have guns. He loves guns. A couple years ago, he shot and killed an intruder. It was a neighbor kid, just sixteen years ago. Turns out the kid wanted to steal some beers from the fridge in his garage. Quincey hangs out in his garage a lot."

"The law didn't punish Quincey?" The vampire found this information interesting. "Allowable savagery?"

"The kid was an intruder. He broke into the garage at three in the morning. Quincey didn't know who it was."

"Besides the guns, what other forms of protection might Quincey have in his home?"

"An attack dog," Lucy said. "A huge Rottweiler named Ajax."

"Named after the mythological Greek hero? Delightful."

"Oh...." said Lucy, confused. "I thought he was named after the kitchen cleaner."

"Can you think of any other information about Quincey's ranch which may be helpful, my dear?"

"He has a lake.... He goes camping by that lake pretty often, all by himself. He likes spending time alone. But he does like company from time to time, like any man."

The vampire smiled. "I take it you and Quincey have been intimate, yes?"

"Yes, lots of times." The escort frowned. "But he doesn't like what I do for a living. He thinks he can catch diseases off me. But I work clean! I'm no skank." A look of sorrow passed over her face. "I help guys. Lonely guys. Men who need somebody who will listen to them. They tell me about their lives, which can be even more intimate than sex."

"Does it thrill you to hear what these men have to say?"

"Sometimes." Lucy sighed heavily. "Most of the time it makes me sad. But I need their money. When I hear their problems, it reminds me that they're still not happy, even though they have a lot of money. They may have the money, but I have the power. The power to make them happy, even if it's just for a little while."

"You and I have a lot in common," the vampire said. "We like to listen to others. I draw strength from the secrets of others. Perhaps you do, too. It's a pity that I'm going to have to kill you. Do you know who Euryale is?"

Lucy shook her head slowly, dreamily. "Noooo...."

"She was the sister of the Gorgon Medusa's sister, and she had a very special power." The vampire touched the medallion that hung from his throat. "She could utter a scream of lament so heartbreaking, it could kill a man. Or a woman."

Dr. Xenos leaned back on the couch and closed his eyes. He took a deep breath, paused, and then opened his mouth. Out came a low, sad tone that grew and grew, building into a rolling thunder of despair. The glass in the windowpanes rattled. Tears rolled down Lucy's cheeks as she clutched her chest.

On and on Dr. Xenos screamed. Lucy opened her mouth, but her low, hollow moan could not be heard over the vampire's anguished cry of doom.

Lucy's eyes rolled back in her head and she fell from the couch, landing softly on the plush white carpeting.

The doctor's screams faded to silence. He stood up and tapped the side of Lucy's head with the toe of his shoe.

No movement.

Dead.

"Good night, sweet harlot," he said, heading for the door.

CHAPTER SIX

The Ice Palace

The Club Contessa
Las Vegas, Nevada

The Ice Palace Casino was a gambling Mecca with a fifty-story high-rise. The entrance of the casino was decorated with thousands of faux ice-crystals, but that wasn't what gave the establishment its name. The interior walls of the casino were covered with actual ice. Refrigerants flowed through pipes in the metal walls, which were regularly sprayed with water, to keep the ice layers refreshed. Rainbow-colored lasers danced continuously across the glittering walls.

While the high-rise had fifty floors, complete with all their crazy Las Vegas goings-on, the real action was on the top floor.

At the very top was an elite nightclub known as Club Contessa. Shaped like an enormous, horizontal wheel, the club slowly rotated, giving the partygoers a spectacular view of Vegas through its many windows. The ice theme used in the casino was also present in the club. The partitions between the windows were covered with ice, as were all interior walls and the ceiling of the club. Patrons accessed the club through a spiral staircase in the center of the club that came up from the lobby in the floor below.

The nightclub was owned by acclaimed pop diva, Contessa Zsa Zsa, more commonly known as simply The Contessa. She was petite—only an inch over five feet—and quite striking. She always wore white, which made her pale complexion shine. Even her hair was as white as snow. Her eyes were as black and shiny as mica and her full lips were as red as the freshly excised heart of a virgin. Her latest release was a high-energy dance hit called "Never Gonna Die Now":

> *"Never gonna die now*
> *Don't even know how*
> *I'm immortal*
> *I'm immoral*
> *Eager lips, cold as ice*
> *Let me freeze you*
> *With a French kiss twice"*

Members of the world's social elite were dying to get into Club Contessa. There were lines around the block every night, but only a few dozen were allowed in at any given time. It was the most dangerous nightspot on the planet, because for one hour every three months, Club Contessa became a disco slaughterhouse.

The night of bloodletting usually took place around closing time on a weekday. It would always be held on a night when there were no top celebrities in attendance: killing off the star attractions was not part of the plan. The giant mirror globe above the center of the club's dance floor would drop like the New Year's Eve ball in Time Square—but instead of a slow descent, it smashed into shards, spearing and slicing the gyrating patrons below.

During that deadly hour, the laser lights weren't just for show. They would burn dancers like pieces of steak left for too long on an outdoor grill. The fog that crept over the lighted floor wasn't just dry-ice vapor. It was, in fact, a mixture of hallucinogenics and laughing gas. Contessa Zsa Zsa was, after all, an entertainer at hard, and always wanted to make sure her guests were having a good time—

right up to the last minute.

Panels in the floor would slide open, revealing gutters for collecting the flowing blood. These gutters led into refrigerated tanks which would keep the blood fresh for the Contessa's blood baths. Soaking in blood kept her skin delightfully smooth and ageless.

When the tri-monthly slaughters were completed, the panels in the floor would close and the Contessa's staff would dispose of the bodies. The refrigeration system within the walls would deactivate. Then the sprinkler system would spray the entire club with hot bleach, dissolving the ice and washing away the blood. The décor was mostly marble, glass and stainless steel, so bleach wouldn't hurt a thing. Then the sprinklers would put the club through several rinse cycles. Blasts of hot air from the specially designed ventilation system would dry out the nightspot.

The refrigeration system would then reactive, and a clubwide spray of water would add fresh new ice to the walls. After a few finishing touches from staff members, the club would be ready for business as usual.

The Contessa performed regularly in both the casino and in the night club. On the club's marble stage was a huge stainless-steel throne. That was where she sat as she performed, flanked on each side of the throne by two huge wolves: a white Arctic wolf named Ulfr and a brown Canadian wolf named Shaitan. Whenever she performed in Club Contessa, it was as though the pop diva was sitting on top of the world—and while that might not have been true, she was indeed sitting at the highest point in the gambling city.

* * * *

"Red Eye!" called the Contessa, summoning her hunchback manservant. Originally she had captured him on a vacation in England and had planned to drain him dry. But she decided he was too ugly for that, so instead she made him her slave. Eventually he was upgraded to assistant, though the roles were about the same. One of his eyes was an attractive sky-blue and the other, which was slighter larger, was a startling dark red—hence his nickname. "Red Eye, come here, please."

Carrying a glass of scarlet liquid, Red Eye shuffled into the chilly office of the pop star's private quarters on the thirteenth floor. She preferred cold temperatures, and enjoyed making snow angels on the floor of her dining room. The manservant's breath drifted forth in white clouds from his thin lips.

"You called, Contessa?" Red Eye said. He shivered, enough though he was wearing a thick black wool coat. "If you ever need to make even more money, you can always rent this place out as a meat locker."

"Silence, munchkin. I asked for that drink five minutes ago."

"My apologies. Here's your blood-orange juice." He handed her the glass and looked up with her with a curious mix of dread and expectancy. "Are you going to hit me? Beat me with that lovely whip of yours?"

"Oh, please. You'd *love* it if I hit you. What kind of punishment would that be?" She drained the glass and handed it back to him. She tousled his thick black hair. "You're okay. But I'm tired of fruit juice. I need the real thing."

"We have a whole tank of blood from the club. Do you want me to get—"

"That cheap crap? That's bathing-quality blood. You know what I want. The *good* stuff. From a virgin."

"A virgin? In Las Vegas, city of ten-thousand whores?" Red Eye rolled his one good eye. "We've hunted down every virgin in town—what few there were!"

"Oh, come now, Red Eye," the Contessa cried. "Think outside the box, as people say these days. Surely a sicko like you can think up new places to find virgins. They don't have to be women, you know. How about religious students? Use your imagination."

"Yes, maybe a shy, pimply seminarian…" Red Eye said, thinking aloud.

She shook her head. "No one with zits. Their lousy hormones will give *me* pimples! I need to maintain a perfect complexion for my fans."

"You *do* have lovely skin, mistress," Red Eye said adoringly. "So milky, so *creamy*. As soft as a baby's bottom."

"There's a thought," the pop diva said. "Babies! All babies are virgins, aren't they?"

"I should *hope* so…" He tapped his chin thoughtfully. "Of course, there's not much blood in a baby. I'm glad you reminded me about male virgins. How about some juicy nerds, fresh from their comic book shops?"

The Contessa smacked her lips. "Ooooh, a nice chubby nerd sounds delicious! Find one with curly red hair and freckles. Gingers are so *tasty.*"

"I guess you've never had a red-haired lover, then," Red Eye said, leering. "Or at least, not for long."

The vampire waggled a red-nailed finger at him. "You should not say such personal things to me. But if you mean 'lover' in the literal sense—one who loves and is loved in return—I've only ever enjoyed the company of one lover. And he did not have red hair."

"That would be Dracula, yes?" Red Eye grinned hugely. "How lucky you were, to have known such a great man! I wish I could have met him."

"You? He would have stabbed you in the head just for looking at him with that insane red eye of yours!" The Contessa laughed, though it sounded more like a hoarse bark. "You're the lucky one. You're lucky you remind me of a red-eyed wolf puppy I once owned. But as for Dracula—! An incredible being. I use the term 'being' because he far stronger and far more intelligent than any mere man. He was like a bolt of lightning in human form. I miss him terribly, and always shall. You don't know what it is like, to have enjoyed the love of one so magnificent—and to realize that you shall never experience that love again. The loneliness cuts through me like a razor blade."

"I know you could never love me," Red Eye said, "but I hope … I hope I relieve your loneliness a *little* bit…?"

The Contessa smiled and nodded. "You do take care of me."

Red Eye returned the smile. "I used to work in the field of emergency care, many years ago. I'm used to tending to the needs of others. And the sight of blood doesn't bother me." He turned and left, off to carry out his orders.

A single blood-red tear rolled down the Contessa's pale cheek.

It froze solid before it hit the floor.

CHAPTER SEVEN

Under A Texas Moon

The residence of Quincey P. Morris
Blanco, Texas

The clear night sky was filled with brilliant stars—more than one would ever see in most polluted urban environments. The full moon cast silver highlights on the midnight landscape.

A shiny red Ford pickup truck was parked off the gravel road. Like many trucks in the area, it featured a gun rack in the rear window, which perfectly legal. In the Lone Star State, one was free to display his or her hunting rifle in the back window.

The truck was parked near a large lake, half-surrounded by trees. About twenty feet from the edge of the lake, a campfire crackled next to an olive-colored tent. Quincey P. Morris sat on a log by the fire, holding a bottle of whiskey in one hand and petting his Rottweiler, Ajax, with the other.

The vampire walked out of the shadows and up to the fire. He wore black jeans and a black t-shirt. The golden medallion, hung from a black vinyl cord around his neck, glittered in the moonlight.

The usually protective, aggressive dog didn't growl as the stranger approached. The vampire had already established eye contact with the animal, lulling it into a deep torpor. The doctor sat at the far end of the log without saying a word.

"I reckoned I'd see you again, Doc," the Texan said, taking another drink from the bottle.

"Really?" The vampire scowled. "We've only met once before. You know little about me. I would have figured my presence here in your native Texas to be quite a surprise."

"*Surprise?*" Quincey said with a laugh. "That's a *Yankee* word. If you wake up in the morning and see that a coyote has jumped up on your bed, you deal with it. Down here, we deal with situations, not surprises."

The vampire moved nearer. "Really? And how do you suppose you would deal with—"

Before he could finish the sentence, Quincey pulled out his Bowie knife and drove it into the vampire's hand, which had been inching closer.

"Son of a bitch!" the vampire cried. He grabbed handle of the knife, and after some twisting and pulling, removed the blade from his hand, which caused it to gush blood. About thirty seconds after the removal of the blade, the wound healed up without leaving a scar. "That was unnecessary," he said with curt irritation. "I cannot afford to waste blood. It is always a precious commodity."

"I knew there was something freaky about you the moment I laid eyes on you," Quincey said. "Back then, I figured you were some kind of swinger-type pervert. But now—" He nodded toward the freshly healed hand. "I guess you're some kind of monster-man, huh? A vampire, maybe, with all your talk about blood? That bat-shit don't fly with me, so why don't you just get the hell off my ranch before I drive a stake through your heart?"

The vampire stared at Quincey. And, Quincey returned the stare, as most people are prone to do when confronted with a compelling gaze. "I *am* a vampire," Dr. Xenos said. "In fact, I have been a vampire many times. The cosmos and its wicked children keep bringing me back. The last time I walked the world, I was confounded by a rather tight group of friends in England. And, it seems the whole batch of you have all been reborn—as friends! Clearly, Fate has given me another chance to destroy the lot of you."

"The lot of … us…?" Quincey said in a sleepy, confused tone.

"Yes. And this time, I have been given the advantage. Your group hasn't caught on to my game yet. I now have additional powers, bestowed upon me by a generous benefactor. Or should I say malefactor? She means me well, but wants me to do great harm to others. And speaking of great harm, that is what is going to befall you shortly. But, you won't be able to do anything about it, because my lovely voice and dazzling green eyes have placed you in a hypnotic trance. Isn't that interesting?"

The Texan nodded. "Interesting…."

"You know what I find *really* interesting?" the vampire said. "Secrets. They have such power … such energy. I want you to tell me your secrets. Your most miserable, wretched, shameful secrets."

"Secrets…" The Texan thought for a moment. "I … I slept with Mina."

"I already know that one. More secrets, please."

"When I was in middle school, I flooded all the toilets in the boy's bathroom. I ran to the next class so I wouldn't get caught. Larry Kramer walked into the mess and was blamed for it and got two weeks of detention."

"Not bad. But I feel you can do better."

"I once got caught playing with myself in the living room when I was a teenager. I was taking a nap on the couch, and when I woke up.... I didn't think anyone was home, so I got to business. I'd looked out the window and the car was gone, so I'd figured mom and dad were off running errands. Turns out, my aunt was borrowing the car and my mom and dad were in the next room. They walked in just as I shouted, 'Blast off!'"

"How amusing," The vampire said with a gentle smile. "More, please."

"At work, sometimes I'll lock the door and touch myself when I should be doing my work. I can't help myself."

"Naughty boy."

"I like camping out here by the lake because I can play with myself for hours, where no one can see. I suppose I could do that in my house, too, but it's sexier, doing it out here in nature."

Dr. Xenos drummed his fingers on the log. "You touch yourself quite a lot, don't you? Let's move into different territory."

Quincey leaned toward the vampire and whispered. "I pick my nose all the time. And, I take laxatives after I eat a lot so I can shit out all the calories."

"Okay..."

"I've been cheating on my taxes for the last decade."

"Aaaahh!" The vampire savored the confession. "That's a nice one. I like that. How much money did you cheat from the government?"

"Lots. Hundreds of thousands. Stashed the money in a Cayman bank account. All tax free, of course."

"Of *course*. Excellent," Dr. Xenos said. "Now tell me, do you have any cattle on this ranch of yours?"

"Certainly. What decent ranch in Texas doesn't have cattle?"

"I see. So you are fairly familiar with bovine creatures. And, apparently they have added to your wealth. What do you know about the Greek myth of the Minotaur?"

"Nothing. I know that Zeus was the top guy among all those old gods, but that's about it."

"The Minotaur was a powerful, brutal creature with the head of a bull on the body of a man," the vampire said. "One of the most ferocious monstrosities that ever lived. The beast lived in the center of the Labyrinth, an elaborate maze built at the command of King Minos of Crete. The Athenian hero Theseus eventually defeated the Minotaur. Are you enjoying my history lesson—or were you thinking about playing with yourself?"

"A little of both," the Texan whispered.

"Horny fellow, aren't you?" the vampire said. "Well, so am I."

With that, Dr. Xenos snorted air from his nostrils and bellowed. His forehead swelled wider, grew higher and thicker—and sprouted curved, shiny-black horns. His eyes turned large and bulbously bovine as thick, bubbling drool poured from his lips.

He lunged forward and stabbed Quincey again and again with his cruel, beautiful horns—first one, then the other, over and over. He stabbed the Texan in the throat, the left eye, the mouth, and the chest, repeatedly. He pierced Quincey's tight abs a dozen times. By the time the vampire was through, the former masturbation addict was sporting more holes than a large block of quality Swiss cheese. The Rottweiler, still lost in a tired daze, licked at the thick puddles of blood clotting on the ground.

Dr. Xenos breathed deeply as he waited for the Minotaur features to recede. When at last he had returned to fully human form, he walked to the lake and began to wash the gore from his clothes and body.

CHAPTER EIGHT

Stone Cold Dead

The Residence of Mina Murray
Elmhurst, Illinois

The black stretch limousine took up most of the driveway. A heavy beat was blasting from inside. It was the tune, "Silly Love Songs," originally recorded by Paul McCartney, but remade by Renfield so that it sounded more horrific than playful. It was the final mix for the rock star's tenth CD, *Marble Tomb for the Bride and Groom.*

Ahmet opened the back door to the car and Renfield stepped out. The rock star wore a black tuxedo, a black cape lined with red satin, a black-silk top hat and white gloves. He looked retro-sinister and oddly charming, like Bela Lugosi done up for a vampire flick. They walked to the front door.

"Ring the bell, please," Renfield said.

The chauffeur rang the bell. No answer.

"Maybe she's in the shower," Ahmet said. He continued to ring for a few more minutes.

Nothing.

"Does the limo have a tire iron?" the man in black asked.

"Sure does, boss. I'll be right back."

A few minutes later, Renfield began prying open the door with the tire iron.

"I can do that, boss," Ahmet said. "Don't mess up your outfit. My old girlfriend Cassandra and I, we used to do a little breaking and entering for kicks while we were dating. She was crazy —all about the thrills."

"How romantic," Renfield said. "But, I'll take care of it, thanks. Haven't done it in a while, I can use the practice."

Renfield soon had the door cracked open. "Mina?" he shouted into the house. "It's me, your old friend Renfield—the Duke of Darkness! Sorry I missed your engagement party!" He paused for a moment, and then added, "And, sorry I broke your door!"

They listened for a response.

Silence.

"I missed your party because I had a rock concert in Sheffield," Renfield shouted. "That Jonathan Harker is sure one lucky guy!"

Still no response.

"It's safe to say, the lady's not home," Renfield said to his chauffeur. "And if she is, she's unable to get to the door. Let's go in."

Renfield led the way. They searched the house room by room, until at last they came to Mina's bedroom.

The door was wide open, and Mina was lying on the bed wearing a light-blue nightgown. Her skin was almost the same shade as her nightwear. The rock star studied her carefully.

"It looks like she's been poisoned," Renfield said. "That won't do for what I had planned. Too much brain tissue has been destroyed, and the nerves—"

"What are you talking about, boss?" Ahmet asked. "What did you have planned?"

"A little ritual I learned from my one of my drummers a few years back. Cool guy. He grew up in Haiti and drank absinthe like most people drink beers." Renfield smiled at the memory. "And not that fake-ass absinthe you see in the supermarkets. He drank the real thing, wormwood and all. That stuff rots your brain and makes you see the Green Fairy."

"Never mind the Green Fairy," Ahmet said. "What about the blue babe?" He nodded at Mina's cyan-hued cadaver.

Renfield sighed. "I'd figured, if anything had happened to her, I could still do that ritual. But we can't do that now, with so much poison in her system." He thought for a moment. "If he got Mina, he probably got Lucy, too. How far is Elmhurst from Downers Grove?"

"About ten miles. If you take 294 to 88, it's about twenty minutes away, at this time of day."

Renfield smiled. "You're a regular GPS tracker, aren't you? Perfect. Drive me to Lucy's place."

A few minutes later, as they were rolling the road, the chauffeur said, "So why would a vampire use poison on his victim? That seems pretty weird."

"I was just thinking about that myself," Renfield said. "You're right, it doesn't make sense. The vampire's methods are beyond me."

"What about your dreams?" Ahmet asked. "Maybe there's some detail in your dreams that you are overlooking."

The rock star gave this concept some thought. "The dreams began after Van Helsing told me about his adventures in fighting Count Dracula. Since those days, he has kept in touch with all the descendants of those who were involved in his fight against the Count. I'm the only one of the descendants he has told—probably because I'm probably the only one who'd believe him. And basically, all my dreams have been much the same—"

"Hey, back up. If Van Helsing fought Dracula back in the day, he couldn't possibly be alive now." Ahmet laughed. "Well, actually, he isn't alive *now*—but he was alive pretty recently."

"Van Helsing was bitten a few times by Dracula," Renfield said. "Van Helsing was able to use his science to stay human, but even so, the vampire's bite had a positive side-effect: a super-long life-span."

"I wouldn't mind that," Ahmet said. "Maybe I can get him to bite me halfway…"

Renfield laughed. "Sorry, it doesn't work that way. Now may I continue with my dreams, if you don't mind…?"

"The floor's yours, boss."

"In the dreams, Van Helsing and the descendants, including myself, are wandering in an enormous castle made of ice or crystal. Down the hallways of the castle swoop two enormous bats—one black as coal with green eyes, the other white with red eyes. The black bat swoops round and round Van Helsing—and with each swoop, Van Helsing shrinks and shrivels until there's nothing left of him. Then the two bats swoop around the rest of us, clawing and scratching at us, shrieking like devils."

"Then what happens?" Ahmet asked.

"That's where the dream stops," Renfield said. "I know the black bat represents Dracula, but I have no idea what to make of the other one."

"Hmmm. Maybe it's some kind of snow-bat, boss."

"A snow-bat? No such thing." Renfield thought for a moment. "But what do I know? I used to think vampires didn't exist. I'm sure we'll find out about the white bat soon enough. Whether we like it or not."

CHAPTER NINE

The Sinmonger

Arthur Holmwood's Movie Studio Office
West Hollywood

Everything about Arthur Holmwood was sloppy: his appearance, the way he worked, and the clumsy couplings he enjoyed with the many starlets he encountered. But that didn't stop him from being a successful horror producer.

The secret to Holmwood's success was simple. First, he would find an available franchise in a fear-film series—usually the third or fourth entry. Then he'd discover some would-be scream-queen with the perfect combination of great cleavage and a piercing shriek. Then he'd add in plenty of gore and topless scenes, and the film would go from clunker to cult classic, all the while making loads of cash.

Arthur's office walls were covered with his movie posters, all featuring a super-cheap monster or villain and a scantily dressed leading lady practically falling out of her tight, skimpy outfit. The titles included *Satan's School for Super-Models (Part 8)*, *Psycho Killer With A Machete (Part 4)*, *Cthulhu's Cheerleaders (Part 2)*, and many more.

The producer wasn't alone. He sat behind his green metal desk, talking with cocktail waitress and fledgling actress Geena Valentyne, whose looks matched all of his previous scream-queens: an hourglass figure, dyed blonde hair with dark roots, and a plastered-on fake smile, complete with dental veneers.

"I assure you," Arthur said, "the rumors of a so-called casting couch in my office have been greatly exaggerated."

Gina sighed with relief.

"It's not a couch at all. It's a futon. Now slip out of that little black dress and I'll pour us some liquid foreplay." So saying, he pulled a bottle of cheap red wine out of the bottom left drawer of his desk.

Gina stood up to unzip the back of her dress. "I should've been a big star by now, but I just haven't had a break yet. I didn't have enough money to get into college to study acting. But I'm a natural actress! Life's been dealing me some crappy cards."

The door of the office slowly opened, but the producer and his starlet were too wrapped up in their conversation to notice.

The producer shrugged. "Feeling down about the hand you've been dealt? Deal another hand. And get that dress off, I don't have all night."

Dr. Xenos cleared his throat. He wore a dark-gray, pinstriped business suit. The medallion hung from his neck on a gold chain.

Gina gasped. "Hey, who's this joker?" she said, staring at the vampire. At this point, her dress was on the floor and she wore only a black satin slip and black-leather pumps. "I don't go for no three-ways. Though he is pretty handsome…" She turned to Holmwood. "Maybe I can do it with him and you can watch. How's that sound?"

"Listen, you ginger creep!" Arthur cried. "Miss Valentyne and I are in the middle of an audition, so why don't you just hit the bricks?"

"'Hit the bricks', Mr. Holmwood?" Dr. Xenos echoed. "Such a quaintly outdated turn-of-phrase. I hope the dialogue in your movies is fresher! I do apologize for interrupting your evening, but I have urgent business with you this evening. It is very much a matter of life and death."

"First things first! Who the hell are you?" Arthur said, annoyed. "And what do you want?"

"I am Dr. Xenos."

"Xenos? Never heard'a ya. I go to Dr. Pretorius. Mostly for diet pills, tranquilizers, and medicinal marijuana."

"Care to share that prescription?" Gina said, smiling prettily. She cast an annoyed glance at Dr. Xenos. "OMG, why are you still here?"

"I don't talk in initials, young lady," the vampire said. "Please put your dress back on and leave. This is a private matter between myself and Mr. Holmwood."

Gina crossed her arms. "Are you going to let him talk to me like that?" she said to the producer.

"Listen, Titty Titty Bang Bang," Arthur said. "Let the adults talk. Maybe this guy's a potential investor. Look at that big chunk of gold he's got dangling around his neck. I'll give you a call if there is another ... opening ... in the near future."

"I can't believe I rescheduled my nail appointment at Lady Wong's for *this!*" she said, grabbing her dress and hurrying out, slamming the door behind her.

"There goes a sweet piece of ass," Arthur said with a laugh. "No talent, but she did have a great scream. Now, what's this matter of life and death?"

"In a previous life, you were a great bother to me, as were your friends. I believe you were the one who put a stake through Lucy's heart. You were a noble adversary ... back then." The vampire stepped closer and began sniffing the air. "Somewhere along the line, you lost that nobility. Now you stink of sin. You *live* for sin. You are a sin addict. A sinmonger."

"Eh, I've been called worse," he said, shrugging it off. "All this previous-life mumbo-jumbo is very interesting, I'm sure. Since we're obviously old pals, you should be happy to invest in one of my movies. Right now, I'm working on a summer blockbuster called *Monster Behind the Wheel*—a sizzling tale of muscle cars, zombies, the works. A guaranteed moneymaker! We'll be rolling in green."

"Green? Like my eyes?" Dr. Xenos said with a smile.

Arthur stared into the vampire's eyes. "Your eyes sure are green. Like, *super*-green. What are you, a leprechaun?"

"Keep looking into my eyes, Mr. Holmwood, you filthy, vice-ridden man. Stare deeply into the green abyss. You are becoming more relaxed. You can barely keep your eyes open."

"Eyes open," the producer repeated sleepily.

"Look into your past. Since your soul in saturated in sin, it shouldn't be hard. Tell me all the ways in which you have violated God's will."

"When I was little, I was always stealing money out of purses," Arthur said. "Any purse I could find! My mom's purse, my sister's purse … even my grandma's purse. The family was always short of money and nobody knew why. I'd spend the money on booze and pot and pretty girls. I financed my first movie, a bargain-basement skin-flick, with a suitcase full of money I found in my grandma's closet. Her life savings! She never trusted banks."

"Stealing from your grandmother," Dr. Xenos murmured. "Delightful! Such exceptionally loathsome behavior."

"Back when I was in college," the producer recalled, "there was this beautiful coed named Cassie Huttlestone. I asked her out on a date once, but she turned me down. I was out of her league, everybody said. One Friday night, she had a fight with her jock boyfriend Ted Simms at a party, and had to walk back to her dorm late at night, all by herself."

"I like where this is going…" the vampire whispered.

"I caught up with her while she was walking up the back stairs to her place. I approached her from behind. I was wearing a hooded sweatshirt and it was really dark—she lived in a crap neighborhood without any streetlights. I threw her to the ground and jumped on-board. I stuffed a glove in her mouth to keep her quiet. Her parents were out getting drunk, like they were every Friday night, so there was no one to interrupt the fun."

"How delightful, that you were allowed to savor the experience."

"Cassie was convinced that Ted had done the deed to get back at her. She didn't want to get him in trouble, so she didn't call the cops. Over the next few days, she talked to Ted and some other folks from the party, and found out he was still at the party at the time of the attack. That's when she called the police—but by then, the baby batter was long gone!"

"Excellent confession! A delicious morsel of sin," Dr. Xenos said.

"A few years later, a girl I was screwing refused to get an abortion, so I paid a guy to push her down some stairs. She died of a broken neck." The producer shook his head angrily. "That stupid bastard wasn't supposed to push her from the *top* of those stairs! I didn't want her to die—she had some inheritance money, she was going to invest in one of my movies!" He sighed deeply, wearily. "Doc, is it true that confession is good for the soul?"

"Yes, it is. But the same doesn't go for the body." The vampire grinned. "Are you familiar with the name Karkinos?"

"No. Who's that, some old Greek millionaire?"

"Karkinos is a crab—"

"Crabs?" Arthur said. "Been there, done that."

"Not that kind of crab, you imbecile. The Greek hero Hercules fought the giant crab Karkinos during one of his Twelve Labors. Hercules dispelled the creature by kicking it with such force, it was propelled into the sky, where it became a constellation."

"So what's with the history lesson?" the producer asked.

"Just an interesting bit of trivia," Dr. Xenos replied. "Now tell me, what is the word that director's say when they want a scene to end?"

The producer cocked his head to one side. "What? You mean, cut? Cut?"

"Don't mind if I do." The vampire instantly raised both hands in the air. As they rose, they began to swell and reshape into huge orange crab claws. He clacked his claws once, twice, and then aimed the vicious, crustacean torture-tools at the producer. Within a few minutes, he'd scissored off the sinful man's lips, fingers, ears, and genitals. As a finishing touch, he sliced open the producer's throat.

"What a pity you can't make any more movies," Dr. Xenos said to the corpse. "You could use your own blood for those gory special effects."

CHAPTER TEN

The Green Girl

The Residence of Lucy Westenra
Downers Grove, Illinois

Again, the black stretch limousine was taking up most of a residential driveway.

Again, Renfield used a tire iron to break open a front door.

This time, upon entering the building, Renfield called out, "Lucy, I'm home!" in a hearty Cuban accent.

"What's with the funny voice?" Ahmet asked.

"You've never seen *I Love Lucy*?" Renfield said.

"Nope."

"Wow."

They found Lucy Westenra lying on the sofa, wearing a fuzzy white robe. Like Mina, she was dead, but instead of blue, Lucy had turned a pale shade of green. Both sides of her head were slathered with clotted blood.

"Looks like he did something to her ears..." Renfield said. "She might be deaf when we resurrect her, but that's not too much of a problem."

"Why's she green like that?"

"All bodies rot in different ways, at different rates," the rock star said. "It might also be an after-effect of the way she died. Maybe it broke a lot of the capillaries near the surface of the skin. But whatever the reason, it's not a problem. Now let's go find some live chickens so we can start the voodoo ritual."

* * * *

It was early evening, and Lucy's naked corpse was covered in chicken blood on the couch. Understandably, the curtains were drawn so that no one could see into the house.

"We killed the chickens, you chanted all that voodoo-hoodoo— still nothing!" Ahmet said, annoyed. "What went wrong?"

"Patience, driver-man," Renfield said. "The moon hasn't fully risen yet. When *that* happens, she will come back to life."

The chauffeur gazed at the bloody, curvaceous body. "You know, before she starts moving around, maybe we could—"

"Ahmet! I'm really surprised at you," Renfield said. "That's a horrible suggestion." He shook his head angrily. "You should have said something *before* we smeared her with chicken blood."

When at last the moon rose, Lucy's body began to jerk, as though she was having a seizure.

"Something's starting to happen, boss!" Ahmet said.

"Of course!" Renfield replied with a grin. "Did you even doubt me? Rock stars can do anything."

Lucy's eyes shot open. She pulled herself up into a sitting position, still twitching and jerking. Renfield picked up her robe, which was laying beside the couch, and draped it over her shoulders.

"Can you hear me, Lucy?" Renfield asked.

The zombie did not respond.

"Whatever killed her must've busted her ear-drums," Ahmet said.

Renfield repeated the question directly in front of Lucy's face. Lucy squinted at him and whispered, "Whaaa...?"

Renfield looked around, spotted Lucy's desk, and went to fetch a pen and paper. He wrote, DID THE VAMPIRE COME TO YOU? on the paper and held it in front of her.

"Vampire...? Dr. Xenos was ... here..." she said in a parched voice. "He made a ... big scream ... so much pain ... pain ... like my head was gonna ... explode...."

"Big scream?" Ahemt said. "Do vampires scream at their victims?"

Renfield shook his head, exasperated. "No. It just doesn't make any sense. This vampire seems to have powers unlike any other creature of its kind."

"Maybe it's not really a vampire," Ahmet said. "Or maybe it's some new kind of monster. Like a Chupacabra."

"Chupacabra's suck *goat's blood,* for Christ's sake." Renfield rolled his eyes. "They don't scream their victims to dead."

"Well, I didn't say it *was* a Chupacabra..."

"Okay, whatever." Renfield turned his attention back to Lucy. He thought for a moment, and the wrote on the paper: CLOSE YOUR EYES. CAN YOU SENSE DR. XENOS? DO YOU KNOW WHERE HE IS?

Lucy closed her eyes. After a few minutes, she opened them. "I think he's … in a coffee shop … at … an airport?" she said. "Yes, an airport. But I don't know the city. I feel that he's … waiting and … that's all. We're too far away, that all I can tell.…"

Renfield frowned. "That doesn't tell us much. That airport could be anywhere." He thought for a moment. "We might need some manpower for this fight. Somebody with a lot of guts. I know just the guy. While we're figuring out how to locate the vampire, we should use that time to go pick him up."

Ahmet nodded. "Sounds like a plan. But first we'd better wash the blood off our lady fair. And find her some decent clothes. We can't have her traipsing around filthy and naked."

"Filthy and Naked," Renfield echoed. "Sounds like a good name for my next band…"

CHAPTER ELEVEN

Three In The Morning

Denver International Airport
Men's Room

Brown slacks dropped around his ankles, Jonathan Harker sat on a toilet in a men's room at Denver International Airport. He was in no hurry to check into the hotel. He felt sad, worried, confused … and constipated.

For two days, he had tried repeatedly to call Mina, Lucy, Quincey and Arthur, and all he ever got was their voice-mails. The flight from New York's John F. Kennedy Airport to Denver had been rough. And to make matters worse, his knotted guts refused to unleash their burden. He fidgeted on the toilet seat as he thumbed the in-flight magazine.

Suddenly, the stall door flew open.

Standing outside of the stall was a handsome man with red hair. He wore a heavy black sweater with a gold medallion pinned over his heart.

"Doctor … Xenos, is it? From our engagement party?" Jonathan said, shocked. "What's going on?" He wanted to get up to shut the stall door, but the surprise of the door flying open had unclenched his sluggish intestines, and he was in no position to rise from his seat.

"Yes, it is me," the vampire said, amused. "Sorry to disturb you, when you have other business at hand."

"Could you … umm, go away for a few minutes?" Harker asked, perturbed and embarrassed. "Now is not a good time. Can't you see that?"

Dr. Xenos shook his head. "Sorry, my friend, but this is very much the *right* time. Look into my eyes."

"Whoa! Is this some kind of crazy come-on? I'm not going to have men's-room sex with you!" Harker stared angrily at the red-haired man—and as he stared, he found himself growing sleepy. "Why am I … so sleepy, all of a sudden? Boy, you sure have green eyes. It's almost as though they were *glowing* green.…"

"You are becoming more and more relaxed," Dr. Xenos said. "Your eyelids feel heavy, as heavy as metal…like lutetium, the heaviest of metals.…"

"Lutetium…?" the pilot repeated in a groggy tone. His eyes slowly closed.

The vampire stepped into the stall and closed the door.

"When you open your eyes," the vampire said, "you will tell me of your sins. Think of me as your priest. This little chamber makes for a cozy confessional."

Harker's eyes opened wide. "I've cheated on Mina, many of times. I've had one-night stands in almost every city I've visited, with plenty of stewardess and other pilots."

"Oh? I didn't realize there were that many female pilots," the vampire noted.

"Who said they were women?" the pilot said.

"I'm not here to judge," Dr. Xenos said. "So, you've been all over the United States, having sex with strangers?"

"And the world, too."

"Excellent. What other sins have you perpetrated?"

"You know, I really would have had men's-room sex with you, if you'd wanted. But I had to act like I didn't, since you must know my friends. You were at that party and all."

"Thank you, I guess," the vampire said.

"I like to gamble," Harker said. "I've lost a lot of money on gambling. But, I usually earn it back, because I'm pretty good at it.

Sometimes, if I've lost money, more money than I can pay back, I'll have sex with the guy who beat me, to pay off the debt."

"That makes you a sort of prostitute," Dr. Xenos observed. "A wonderfully unexpected sin!"

"Oh, I've let lots of guys do me for money," Harker said. "I don't even ask them to wear a condom. I'm lucky I haven't contracted any diseases. Like I said: I'm a gambler."

"What other sins can you add to your roster?"

"I like vodka enemas," Harker said, matter-of-factly. "The body absorbs the alcohol much faster than way. Sometimes I'll eat a whole pie and then stick my finger down my throat to barf it back up, so it doesn't make me fat. If I'm in a strange city, I'll hit the bars in drag, and I don't want to get fat because then I won't be able to fit into any of my outfits."

"Oh, my…" the vampire purred. "You really are a tasty storehouse of sins! Bravo, my friend! Any more…?"

"I like being spanked," Harker said. "And choked. Oooooh, I really liked being choked. But not too much: I can't go to work with bruises around my neck."

"You like being choked, eh?" the red-haired man said. "Well then, this is your lucky night. By any chance, have you ever heard of Scylla?"

"No. What is that, some kind of sports car?"

"Not quite," the vampire said. "Scylla is a rather famous monster, featured in that classic work, *The Odyssey*. Scylla is also the most irresistible of monsters: the more you fight it, the more it draws you in. But I think it would be easier to show you, than to tell you.…"

The vampire quickly pulled off his sweater. From out of his back and sides sprouted six fleshy tentacles, each tipped with a long, toothy head. Each head looked like a bony cross between a greyhound and a serpent. The heads all had many sharp, yellowish fangs—triple rows of them, like a shark. Green scales grew out of the surface of the tentacles. The dog-headed tentacles wrapped around Harker's body and began to squeeze. One tentacle curled around his neck and flexed tightly, until the pilot could no longer breath.

Then the vicious canine heads began to bite.

The vampire enjoyed seeing the look of hideous bliss on the pilot's face.

Afterward, Dr. Xenos washed up in the men's room sink, slipped on his sweater, and strolled back out into the airport.

CHAPTER TWELVE

Home On The Range

The Residence of Quincey P. Morris
Blanco, Texas

The red truck was still parked by the lake. Twenty feet from the edge of the water, a half-dozen coyotes feasted on the remains of Quincey P. Morris.

The helicopter carrying Renfield, Ahmet, and Lucy landed so near the tent, the wind from the whirling blades blew the canvas and ropes right off the tent-stakes. Four coyotes ran off, snarling. The trio got out of the whirlybird and walked over to Quincey's corpse.

"Shoo! Shoo!" the Goth rock-star shouted at the remaining coyotes. The scavengers ignored him as they fought over a chunk of thigh-meat. Renfield took out his Ruger LCP Pistol and shot twice into the air, scaring off the last two beasts. "Damn!" he said. "I figured Quincey would be here. He loved this lake. But the vampire got him first."

Lucy picked up a forearm and began to gnaw on it. No one tried to stop her.

Renfield grabbed Quincey's torn, battered head by the hair. "Alas, poor Quincey! I knew him well," he said. "A fellow of infinite jest, of most excellent fancy...."

"What the hell are you talking about?" Ahmet asked.

"Just paying tribute to an old friend, the Shakespeare way," Renfield said with a sigh, tossing the head aside. "Not enough of him left to bother raising him from the dead. We have to come up with a new game plan. We can't keep on chasing shadows across the country. This is getting us nowhere fast."

"I hear you, boss. What do you suggest?"

"Let's pay a visit to Dr. Seward. Maybe he can hypnotize Lucy ... drill into her psyche and get more information out of her, before her brain rots away."

"Good idea, boss." Ahmet stared at Lucy, who was now chewing on a dusty rib. "This trip wasn't a total waste of time. We were able to fill Lucy's belly."

The three walked back to the helicopter and were soon airborne again.

CHAPTER THIRTEEN:

The Doctor Will See You Now

The Office of Dr. John Seward
St. Louis, Missouri

Dr. John Seward stood at the window, lost in thought. His practice was located on the top floor of his office building, and in the distance, he could see the Gateway Arch, shining in the moonlight. He savored the view and a glass of aged Scotch whiskey simultaneously. In a corner of the office, a cherrywood grandfather clock clicked and clacked.

Seward only drank whiskey out of real glass, never plastic. It seemed that whenever he drank alcohol out of plastic, he could taste the difference. Perhaps the alcohol dissolved a bit of the plastic into the drink. The faint chemical taste was probably all in his imagination, but even so, it decreased his enjoyment, and he wasn't about to let *that* happen.

Lost in thought, Seward didn't notice Dr. Xenos as he slipped silently into the office.

"Good evening, Sea Weed," the vampire said.

"Quincey? I've been trying to get a hold of you!" Dr. Seward turned around and gasped when he saw the red-haired man standing in front of his desk. "What the—? You're that fellow at I met at Mina and Jonathan's engagement party. Doctor ... Zorro, is it?"

"Xenos. Dr. Xenos."

"Oh yes, I remember now. This is quite a surprise! Now tell me, why did you call me Sea Weed? That's what my friend Quincey calls me. Did he tell you that?"

"Yes, he did. Of course, Quincey and I had a difference of opinion recently. I was certainly a thorn in his side."

"I see…" Seward stared at his unexpected visitor. He noticed that the red-haired man wore a gold medallion on a thin gold chain around his neck. "That's quite a chunk of gold you've got there."

Dr. Xenos smiled. "I've had it for years. I wear it all the time."

"So tell me, why exactly are you here?" Seward asked.

The vampire walked to the side of the desk, so that he was only a few feet away from the doctor. "I was wondering if you could take a look at my eyes."

"Your eyes? Dr. Xenos, I'm a psychologist, not an optometrist."

"Really? My mistake." He smiled warmly. "Well, I did travel quite a long way to be here. Can you take a quick look anyway?"

"But… Aren't you a doctor, too? I have no idea what is going on right now!" Suddenly Seward laughed heartily. "Wait a minute! Did Quincey put you up to all this? Are you leading up to some kind of crazy joke?"

Dr. Xenos nodded. "Yes. Absolutely hilarious."

"Well then, what the hell. I'll look into those big shiny peepers of yours!" Seward drew closer to Dr. Xenos and looked into his eyes. "They sure are green. You have the greenest eyes I've ever seen. If I didn't know better, I'd think they were getting greener and shinier, right now!"

"Green, the color of envy," the vampire whispered. "The color of evil. Just stare into the bright green abyss."

"Bright green abyss…" Seward repeated sleepily.

"Tell me, Sea Weed. Are you a good boy, or a bad boy? Tell me about your sins."

"My sins…?"

"Yes. Your sins, your immoral acts, your transgressions against divine law. Tell me now.…"

"When I was ten years old, I really wanted the Captain Turbo action figure. My parents wouldn't buy for me and it was way too expensive for my puny allowance. So I had Grandpa take me to the toy store one weekend … it was winter, and I was wearing one of those big, quilted kid's coats. While Grandpa was in the bathroom, I stuck the action figure into my coat. I shoplifted it.…"

"Excellent!"

"No, wait. That's not the end of the story. At the last minute, I decided against stealing it. I took the action figure out of my coat and gave it to the clerk. He reported it to his manager, who called my parents. I was grounded for a month."

"Oh…" Dr. Xenos sighed with exasperation. "That's not really a sin. You didn't do the crime, but you still confessed. Any others?"

Dr. Seward was silent for a full minute. The grandfather clock kept ticking and ticking.

"In high school, I was really bad at Algebra. A kid in my class named Kenny stole the answers from the teacher's desk and made copies for everyone…."

"Is that so…?" Dr. Xenos whispered, delighted.

"Yes. But, I didn't take the copy he made for me. I decided, I'd rather get a B for honesty than an A-plus for cheating."

Dr. Xenos pouted. "Oh, come now. You can do better than that!"

"I do like to have a nip every now and then," Seward said, holding up his glass. "But, just a bit. I don't like to get drunk. I really just drink fine whiskey for the flavor."

The vampire grew angry. "You are a rather boring man, Dr. Seward! As boring as sea weed! In fact, sea weed is much more interesting than you!"

"I don't have time for sin," Seward said. "My life is all about work. bout helping others. I *like* helping others."

"But without any sins, I cannot feed the Hydra!" Dr. Xenos cried.

"I have no idea what that means…." Seward said. "This is all really confusing."

Dr. Xenos thought for a moment.

"You're right. This *is* a confusing situation," the vampire said. A smile spread slowly across his face. "How does one alleviate confusion? With simplicity, of course. With that in mind, I'll take care of you the old-fashioned way."

With that, the vampire lunged at Dr. Seward, sinking his fangs into the psychologist's neck.

As he sucked hungrily at the muscular neck, his eyes happened to fall upon something colorful on the doctor's desk. It was a brochure for the Ice Palace Casino in Las Vegas. The cover showed a bevy of beautiful young ladies in sequined evening gowns. The girls sipped on cocktails and flirted with leering male admirers in loud blazers.

Tacky. Humans were such tasteless sheep. Except, of course, for their rich, red blood—*that* was tasty.

After he'd finished his liquid dinner, he pushed the doctor's body to the floor and then picked up the brochure. He did enjoy the occasional game of chance. Perhaps a trip to this casino might make for an amusing weekend. He opened the brochure and—

There! There she was!

That pale skin, those eager coal-black eyes, those scarlet lips—there could be no mistake! It was her: the Countess Erzsébet Dolingen—and before that, Countess Elizabeth Bathory.

The love of his life!

The brochure said the beautiful woman was the Contessa Zsa Zsa, a pop star who performed regularly at her own club, located in the fifty-story high-rise adjacent to the casino.

Not only had his beloved survived the centuries, she'd even managed to thrive in a world filled with meddling do-gooders dedicated to hunting down and exterminating vampires.

His mission of vengeance would have to wait. After all, he had all the time in the world to track down his enemies. It was now time to track down his beloved.

Next stop: Las Vegas!

* * * *

The helicopter landed in the parking lot outside of Dr. Seward's office building.

Renfield, the zombie that was once Lucy, and Ahmet all exited the chopper and crossed to the entrance of the building.

"I...I can feel him..." Lucy said in a low, raspy tone. "He's in this building."

"Shit!" Renfield cried. "The bastard's always one step ahead of us! Seward's probably dead already."

"You heard the zombie!" Ahmet said. "The vampire is still in the building. Maybe we can still catch him. Do we have anything to chop his head off...? Hey, maybe we can hold him up under the chopper and let the blades cut his head off!"

"That's the craziest thing I ever heard!" Renfield said. "And that's why I like it. Come on, let's go get him."

A security guard came out of the building. He was a tall, thin man with a pockmarked complexion and a name badge that read PERKINS. "What's going on out here?" he said in a high, nasal voice.

"You can't just park a helicopter out here!"

"You're probably not going to believe this," Renfield said, "but there is a vampire loose in your building and we have reason to believe that he is after Dr. Seward."

The guard frowned. "You're right, I don't believe you."

The rock star pulled his wallet out of his pocket and brought forth eight hundred-dollar bills. "Do you believe me now, Perkins?"

The guard stared hard at the money. Then he reached out, placed his hand over the bills and pulled them from Renfield's loose grasp.

"Come on, friend," Perkins said with a wink, slipping the money into his shirt pocket. "Let's go check on the doc. Better make sure that vampire keeps his fangs to himself."

The group entered the building and crossed to the elevators. A moment later, they were on their way to the top floor. "You're lucky it's after hours," the guard said. "So what's really going on? Is this some kind of rich weirdo prank?" He pointed at Lucy. "You sure did a great job on her make-up. It looks totally real!"

"This," Renfield said, laying a hand on Lucy's cold shoulder, "is an honest-to-goodness zombie. We're using her to track the honest-to-goodness vampire who killed her."

The guard wrinkled his nose. "I'm starting to smell her… I think I believe you!"

Ahmet tapped the guard on the shoulder. "Don't get shook, okay? Just work with us and everything will be okay. Believe it or not, we're the good guys."

The elevator door opened and the group walked out onto the top floor. Perkins let them to Dr. Seward's suite, No. 66. There was no need to knock, since the door was wide open. Within, they saw Dr. Seward sprawled in a pool of his own blood.

"Oh, hell," Perkins said.

"Very strange…" Renfield said, examining the twice-punctured neck. "Dr. Seward was bitten."

"So?" Ahmet said. "What's so strange about that? A vampire did the deed."

Renfield took a pen and sheet of paper from the doctor's desk and wrote, WHERE IS THE VAMPIRE NOW, LUCY? He then handed the message to the zombie. Upon reading it, she closed her eyes for a moment.

"He … he's very near. He's in this building, riding down in a service elevator," she said. "He's thinking about a woman in Las Vegas … a beautiful blonde called The Contessa. He misses her … he loves her! She's a vampire, too!"

"The Contessa? A vampire?" Renfield cried. "That's incredible! She's a big star—almost as big as me! Shes a headliner at one of the clubs out there."

"*Almost* as big as you?" Ahmet said. "She's *way* bigger than you! She's an international superstar!"

"Thanks for the vote of confidence," Renfield said. "Meanwhile, we're wasting time. We need to find that bloodsucker *now*." He turned to the security guard. "Perkins, where's that service elevator?"

"Follow me," Perkins said heading toward the door. "I'll lead you to it."

The team followed the guard down the hall and around a corner, where they found the service elevator. As they headed down to the ground floor, Ahmet said, "We may not catch up to him. He's had too much of a head start."

"You know, we've been running around the country, chasing this guy, like chickens with the heads cut off," Renfield said. "I wish I knew how he's able to get around so quickly."

"At least we're getting closer," the chauffeur said. "And we know his next stop. And there's no way we'd know that, if it weren't for Lucy."

"Hey, look at this!" Perkins said. He picked up a golden disk and a thin broken chain from the floor of the elevator, which was covered with grey carpeting, torn in spots. He handed the medallion and chain to Renfield.

Lucy touched the medallion. "That belongs to Dr. Xenos," she croaked in dry, raspy tones. "It gives him … great power. But he is … obsessed with the Contessa … he doesn't realize that it's lost."

Renfield examined the image on the front of the medallion. "It's a snake with nine heads— the Hydra from Greek mythology. What kind of power could a vampire get from this?"

At that moment, the elevator doors opened. Renfield pocketed the medallion and the chain. The crew rushed out, looking down every adjacent hallway as they headed for the exit. Outside of the building, Renfield, Ahmet, and Perkins searched the grounds, but no one was around. Lucy gnawed on a roadkill squirrel she'd found in the parking lot.

"We'd better head for Las Vegas," Renfield said. "At least we've got that gold thingabob. That might come in handy." He patted Perkins on the back. "Thanks for your help tonight, buddy."

"Wish I could go with you!" Perkins said. "But, I'm going to have to tend to things here, what with Dr. Seward being dead and all. What am I supposed to tell the police?"

Renfield pulled out his wallet and fished out more hundred-dollar bills. "I don't care what you tell them, so long as you leave us out of it."

CHAPTER FOURTEEN:

The Thirteenth Floor

The Ice Palace Casino
Las Vegas, Nevada

In the lobby of the Ice Palace Casino, Dr. Xenos stared at the elevator's decorative gold buttons. The elevator led up through the fifty-foot high-rise. Where, he wondered, in this towering structure should a search for the Countess begin...? Or rather, the Contessa. That's what she called herself these days. He would have to call her that, too.

A smile stretched slowly across his face. The thirteenth floor, of course. The Contessa used to say that thirteen was her lucky number.

He regarded the M button between 12 and 14. Many skyscapers used M for the thirteenth floor. The M usually stood for either Mezzanine or Maintenance. In this case, he mused, he hoped M stood for Magnificent. He pressed the button.

Nothing, even after waiting a full minute. He thought for a moment, than punched the button thirteen times.

The elevator rose and after a few minutes, stopped at the thirteenth floor. But, the doors did not automatically open. The red-haired man stared at the control panel. *Now* what was he supposed to do?

Above the control panel was a pattern of small metal studs. Most looked like small blazing suns, surrounded by spiky rays, while others looked like leaves, snowflakes and flowers.

He thought for a moment. The Contessa adored winter weather....

He pressed each of the snowflakes.

The elevator doors opened and Dr. Xenos stepped into a winter wonderland—situated in a high-rise in the middle of Las Vegas.

He looked around. The windows were etched with a lacework pattern of frost, while the hallways and furniture were heaped with snow. Golden-eyed wolves glared at him from the couches, but they kept their distance. They knew a superior predator when they saw one.

None of this was a surprise to the vampire. The Contessa was adept at many different forms of dark magic. For her, summoning winter winds was a simple matter. Las Vegas was a city filled with violent crime and vice, and since she slept during the day, she probably wished to keep multiple layers of protection between her and those who might wish to harm her while she rested. No doubt she also enjoyed the company of the wolves during her waking hours.

The vampire walked down a frost-lined hallway, looking into each doorway along the path. It was a beautifully furnished penthouse with a décor of steel and black velvet. He turned a corner and found himself facing huge double doors. The snow was pushed away from the front of the doors, so apparently they had been opened recently. He pulled at a door and it opened easily, revealing a spacious dining room.

At the head of the long steel-and-glass dining table sat the object of his undead desires. Contessa Zsa Zsa, also known over the centuries as Countess Erzsébet Dolingen and Countess Elizabeth Bathory.

Truly, she hadn't changed at all over the years. As always, her flawless skin and shining hair were both as white as snow. Her eyes remained as black as the night sky. Her full lips were still far redder than any rose.

"At last!" Dr. Xenos cried. "At long last!"

The Contessa rose from her chair, speechless. She rushed into his arms and they shared a passionate embrace. She covered his face with kisses, smearing his lips and cheeks with bright red lipstick.

"It's you!" she cried. "You've got red hair now, but I'd know you anywhere. It's *you!* I—I'd given up on you! I though you were dead!"

"Well, *of course* I'm dead!" the Count said with a laugh. "But I did cease to exist for a while. Still, nothing can keep me away from you. Absolutely nothing."

"Let us celebrate!" said the Contessa. She turned toward the door. "Red Eye!"

No response was forthcoming.

"*Red Eye!*" the Contessa shrilled, louder and with a distinctively furious edge.

The hunchback shambled into the room. "My apologies, Contessa." He noticed the red-haired man. "Oh, I see we have a guest! I apologize again for not seeing you in, sir. I was preparing dinner for the wolves and the goat-skinning was at a critical stage."

"Enough with the excuses. Two glasses of the finest blood we have," the Contessa said. "*Immediately!* If you're not careful, I'll be feeding *you* to the wolves."

Red Eye nodded nervously and hurried out of the room.

The Contessa giggled. "I'm not really mad at him. I just like to make him squirm."

CHAPTER FIFTEEN

What To Do About Lucy

Cassandra's Desert Souvenirs
Outside of Las Vegas, Nevada

"We've got to do something about Lucy," Ahmet said. He began to lower the helicopter toward a shabby ranch-style building five miles outside of Las Vegas. Though it was still early morning, the sun was already heating up the tight confines of the chopper. "She's really starting to stink, and she's three shades greener than a shamrock. We can't go walking around in downtown Las Vegas with a putrefying zombie. I have a friend in that building down there who can help us."

Above the entrance of the building was a sign that read CASSANDRA'S DESERT SOUVENIRS, spelled out in red rattlesnake letters. While Ahmet parked the chopper in the empty parking lot, a reed-thin, black-haired woman in a black wedding gown came strolling out of the building. Her lean, pretty face was slathered with thick

Goth make-up—from lipstick and lipliner to eye-shadow and eye-liner and five different shades of rouge.

"Oh my God!" she screamed as the crew unmounted from the helicopter. "Ahmet, I haven't seen you in like, forever! At least three or four years. And you brought Renfield! I can't believe it! I have all his CDs!"

"Everybody, I'd like you to meet Cassandra Rambling," Ahmet said. "Cassandra, meet everybody. We've got a job for you that—"

"Hey, what's wrong with that lady?" Cassandra said. "Oh my God, is she a zombie? I've never seen a zombie before! Is she going to be okay?"

"Well, no, she's *never* going to be okay…" Ahmet said. "We need for you to pretty her up so what she can be presentable in public. It'll take a while, so the rest of us need to take a nap while you're doing that. Does all that sound okay?"

"Whoa!" Cassandra cried. "I'm not going to use-up a shitload of quality make-up on a corpse for nothing! What do you think I am, an undertaker?"

"I'll give you two-thousand dollars in cash to do it," Renfield said, matter-of-factly.

The Goth woman smiled. "Welcome to Cassandra's House of Zombie Make-Overs."

* * * *

In the master bedroom, Dr. Xenos and the Contessa held each other in her huge, cushion-laden bed after yet another hour-long session of feverish lovemaking.

"That was marvelous," the Contessa said with a sigh. She gazed at her lover with open curiosity. "So tell me. Why do you have red hair now?"

"Like I said before: I was reborn," he said. "Things change when a person is reborn. Like hair color, fingerprints all that. A witch named Melina brought me back to life. She gave me—" He put a hand to his neck. Then he felt around his throat with both hands. "The medallion! It's gone!"

He jumped out of bed and searched through his clothes, piled at the foot of the bed. "Where is it? Where did my medallion go?"

The Contessa frowned. "Medallion? What are you talking about?"

"Did you see a large, circular gold disk on a chain around my neck when I got here?" Dr. Xenos said.

The Contessa shook her head.

"Hell." The vampire sat on the edge of the bed. "The chain must have broke… But when? Where…?"

"Is it really all that important?" The Contessa said. "It's only jewelry, right?"

"The medallion is everything to me!" the red-haired man cried. "I draw enormous strength from it. The witch who brought me back to life gave it to me. She used it in the ritual. I was reborn in the body of a dead woman."

"Your second mother was a corpse?" The Contessa smiled. "The blackest of black magic!"

"The medallion gives me the powers of nine monsters from Greek mythology," Dr. Xenos said. "It draws energy from the sins of others. One round of confessions from a mortal can power several transformations. But I have to be wearing it to draw on that energy."

"This Melina must have belonged to the Cult of the Hydra," said the Contessa. "A very small, elite sect. Their beliefs create a bridge between Satanism and Greek mythology. They see great evil as a noble virtue. No wonder she brought you back to life. In her eyes, you were up among the saints. When did you last see this medallion of yours?"

He thought for a moment. "I know I was wearing it in Dr. Seward's office. He even mentioned it. And after that… I don't know."

"Don't worry about it," the vampiress said. "We'll find it, eventually. You said it was made of gold, so it's not like anyone is going to discard it. It may take time, but we'll track it down."

Dr. Xenos nodded.

"So which powers from what Greek monsters does the medallion give you?" the Contessa asked. "Can it make you turn people into stone, like the Medusa?"

"Certainly," Dr. Xenos said. "I used the medallion's power to turn Abraham Van Helsing to stone. Afterward, his many sins gave me enough power to sprout the tentacles of Scylla. I used those tentacles to crush his stone remains to rubble."

"Fascinating!" the Contessa said. She wagged a finger at his crotch. "Can you turn into the Minotaur—and when you do, are you hung like a bull?"

"I can take on the Minotaur's powers and grow massive horns," Dr. Xenos said, "but that's all that becomes massive."

The Contessa shrugged. "No problem, you're big enough as it is. What other monsters are on the menu?"

"Well, let's see… I can exhale a poisonous breath, like the Hydra. I can issue a killing scream, like the Medusa's sister, Euryale. I can grow giant claws, like those of Karkinos, the crab that fought Hercules. I can sprout the giant bird-wings of a Harpy and fly faster than most jets. I've been using those wings a lot lately, to fly from death to death."

"Is that how you got to Las Vegas?" the Contessa asked.

"No, Dr. Seward didn't have any sins to share, so I knew I wouldn't have the power. I didn't even bother *trying* to grow the wings. That's probably why I didn't miss the medallion until now. I had to take a commercial flight."

"That adds up to seven monsters," the Contessa said. "What are the last two?"

Before Dr. Xenos could answer, a knock sounded at the door. The vampire crawled back under the bedsheets.

"Come in, Red Eye," the Contessa said. "Whatever it is, make it quick."

The hunchback entered the room. "Sorry to interrupt. I wanted to let you know, a potentially dangerous character is loose in the hotel."

"Dangerous? In what way?" the Contessa asked. "Is it a terrorist?"

"No, it's a zombie. A female zombie. I took a picture with my cellphone." So saying, Red Eye handed the vampiress his phone.

The Contessa examined the image. It depicted a pretty, busty blonde with heavy make-up. She wore a tight black dress and bright pink fishnet stockings. "Zombie? It's just another Goth, tackier than most. I don't see anything wrong with her." She then handed the phone to Dr. Xenos. "What do you think?"

"That's Lucy!" the red-haired man said. "I killed her back in Illinois. I blew out her ears! How can this be?"

The Contessa turned to Red Eye. "She doesn't *look* like a zombie. How were you able to tell?"

"I saw her in the lobby with a couple of guys," Red Eye said.

"She's not very steady on her feet. Somebody went to a lot of trouble to hide the fact that she's a zombie. They piled on the make-up and the perfume, but they still couldn't hide the stench. Not completely. Plus, she's dripping pus. Not constantly, but the maintenance staff will still need to work overtime to clean up after her. Security wanted to kick them out, but I told them I needed to observe them."

"It seems you have enemies who have followed you here," the Contessa said to her lover. "Fairly powerful enemies, too, if they can bring the dead back to life. But no matter: we'll send that zombie and her allies straight to Hell."

"Not so fast, my darling," Dr. Xenos said. "They may have my medallion."

"What do you suggest we do?" the Contessa said.

"Wait. Let them make the first move. We have the advantage since we know they're here. They cannot take us by surprise." Dr. Xenos handed the cellphone to Red Eye. "You did good."

"Thank you, sir!" Red Eye said, grinning.

The Contessa pinched her lover's forearm. "Don't encourage him."

CHAPTER SIXTEEN

Attack From Above

The Club Contessa
Las Vegas, Nevada

"This doesn't feel right," Renfield said as he set the bazooka inside the helicopter.

"What do you mean?" Ahmet said. "Here ya go." He handed Renfield the flame-thrower to add to their flying arsenal.

"I mean, we scoped out the whole high-rise and nobody screwed with us." He shook his head. "Nobody said, 'Hey, your ladyfriend is leaking liquid-stink with every other step.' People were complaining like crazy. Why didn't Security toss us out?"

"Well, a place like that gets a lot of hookers," Ahmet said matter-of-factly. "Maybe leaky skanks are more common than you realize."

"Truuuuue.... I hadn't thought of that. Speaking of our leaky

Lucy, shall we bring her along? She's getting pretty rank. She might be too much of a distraction."

"Yeah, a distraction for *them*," the chauffeur said. "We're used to the odor. They're not."

Renfield nodded. "We'll hit 'em with everything we've got."

* * * *

The helicopter landed on the roof of the Club Contessa at midnight. The plan was to rush in among the late-night revelers, separate Dr. Xenos and the Contessa from the herd, reduce them to ashes with the flamethrower, and then saturate the ashes with holy water. At some point, they hoped the two vampires would manifest some sort of horrific supernatural behavior, so that witnesses would quickly realize that Renfield and Ahmet were valiant monster-slayers, not insane murderers.

Renfield, Ahmet and Lucy climbed out of the helicopter. Ahmet took up the bazooka and Renfield grabbed the flamethrower. Lucy was already armed with a seriously severe super-stench.

Red Eye was waiting for them at the door that led down into the club.

"Welcome to the Club Contessa, the premier nightspot for children of the night," the hunchback said. "My master and mistress asked me to escort you down to the club. We saw your helicopter approaching the building, and were quite impressed. You're certainly the most *aggressive* party-crashers we've ever encountered."

"This can't be good," Renfield whispered to his chauffeur.

The hunchback led the trio down the stairs and through a winding hallway to the empty dance floor of the Club.

The club's marble stage was dominated by a stainless-steel throne, upon which sat Dr. Xenos, with the Contessa on his lap. Ulfr, the white Arctic wolf, stood by one side of the throne, and Shaitan, the brown Canadian wolf, stood by the other.

"Well, if it isn't Renfield the Goth sensation!" the red-haired man said. "I have all your CDs. I use them as drink coasters. I see you somehow managed to bring Lucy back from the dead. My dear Lucy, what *is* that heavenly perfume you're wearing?"

"She can't hear you," Renfield said. "She's deaf."

"Oh yes, I forgot. My bad!" Dracula said, slapping his forehead with a broad smile. "I'm in a festive mood this evening. We should start this party by sacrificing a virgin. Any candidates in the room?"

Red Eye instinctively raised his hand, than brought it down quickly. "Uh-oh! I'm out of here!"

"Calm down, Red Eye," said the Contessa. "He's joking. No one's sacrificing anybody."

But, the distraught hunchback wasn't listening. He turned and began to run toward the staircase, colliding with the zombie Lucy who stood just a few feet behind him.

"Out of my way, you filthy pus-bucket!" the hunchback said, pushing Lucy to the floor.

Enraged, Lucy rose to her feet and grabbed Red Eye by the hair. She dragged him to the spiral staircase and with a mighty heave, pushed him over the railing. The hunchback managed to catch hold of a banister as he fell down the stairwell.

Lucy, however, was thrown off-balance by her tussle with Red Eye. She staggered awkwardly for a moment—and then one of her heels suddenly snapped. The zombie toppled forward, right down the stairs. When she hit bottom, her rotten belly ruptured, spraying the lobby with black blood and yellow pus.

The Contessa jumped off her lover's lap and moved closer to the staircase so she could see what had happened. She laughed when she saw her assistant clinging to the banister. "Red Eye! This is no time for dilly-dallying. Stop hanging around and serve your mistress!"

"Forget about him," Dr. Xenos said. "It's time for lady's choice! Who do you want? The skinny Goth singer or his stupid helper?"

"I never eat the help! Just ask Red Eye. But, I've always had a thing for Goth boys," Contessa said with a sigh.

"In his previous life," Dr. Xenos said, "this Renfield fellow was my insane assistant. It's interesting that he's trying to kill me now. The maniac has become the hero ... and I hate heroes. You know, my dear Contessa, his music is very popular with young people. He's your nearest competitor on the music scene!"

The blonde vampire's pretty smile turned down into an ugly frown. "Oh, yes.... Now that you mention it, I think I've heard of this no-talent hack."

Red Eye used all his upper-body stretch to pull himself over the banister. Years of lifting the Contessa's heavy luggage had given him strong arms. He ran to the bottom of the stairs as fast as he could. He didn't like the Contessa's new companion. It was time to find a new gig. Vegas held plenty of opportunities for an enterprising weirdo with big dreams.

He was ready to get in the elevator when he saw something shiny and red out of the corner of his eye. It was an axe, hanging in a glass case under a sign that read: FOR EMERGENCIES ONLY. A small hammer dangled from a chain next to the case.

Red Eye ogled the axe adoringly. He loved playing with shiny new toys. He found them absolutely irresistible.

Time to party.

CHAPTER SEVENTEEN

Red Eye's Revenge

The Club Contessa
Las Vegas, Nevada

Renfield stared down the stairwell at Lucy. She was still twitching, despite the fact that she'd pretty much fallen apart. He raised the flame-thrower and turned toward Dr. Xenos—

But quick as a lightning strike, the vampire was already at his side.

Dr. Xenos grabbed Renfield by the throat. "You've saved me the trouble of hunting you down," he said. "And for that, I thank you. Now, be a good boy and look into my eyes."

"Look into … your eyes?" The Goth pop star said. He could not help but stare into the green depths of the vampire's eyes …. twin swirling galaxies of evil, quickly and thoroughly mesmerizing him. "Wow, they sure are green … the greenest green I've ever seen…" He dropped the flame-thrower without giving it a second thought.

"Boss, snap out of it!" Ahmet said, aiming the bazooka at the red-haired man. "He's pulling some crazy hypnosis shit on you."

"Lower your weapon," the Contessa said to Ahmet. "They're too close together for you to do any blasting with that thing."

"Your sins!" Dr. Xenos cried, staring deeply into Renfield's eyes. "Tell me your sins! I first want to know what you've stolen."

"Stolen...?" Renfield said with a laugh. "I've stolen so many things, we'd be here for years! I've stolen the virtue of many a groupie Goth girl, that's for sure. Sometimes two at a time. If you're willing to go back a few years, I've stolen cash, credit cards, jewelry, leather jackets, TV sets, booze, drugs, cars ... you name it, I've swiped it. You could even say I've stolen a life. The guy was a crazy drug dealer who'd sampled a few too many of his own wares. It was self-defense, but I never reported it to the police."

"Such delicious, powerful sins!" the red-haired man murmured. "I'm also interested in what you've stolen *recently*. I feel the presence of my property on your person..."

The vampire reached into Renfield's vest pocket and pulled out the gold disk.

"I didn't steal it," Renfield said. "We found it in a service elevator in an office building."

"A service elevator...?" Dr. Xenos murmured. "That must have been after my visit with Dr. Seward. No matter! I have my property back, and you have energized it with your sins. And what sins! A regular smorgasbord of wickedness. Thanks for keeping it short but sweet!"

Renfield shook his head violently, as though waking from a horrible dream. "What—? What just happened?"

"Seek cover, Renfield!" Ahmet cried, raising the bazooka and aiming it at the vampire. The pop-star quickly assessed the situation and did as he was told, flinging himself behind a nearby bartender's station. The chauffeur pulled the trigger and sent a missile flying at Dr. Xenos.

A blinding flash and loud explosion filled the club as the vampire was engulfed in flame. The force of the explosion shattered many of the club's large windows.

When the smoke cleared, Dr. Xenos was still standing.

His clothes were burned away, revealing a body covered with thick golden fur. He held the golden medallion triumphantly over his head.

"What the Hell—?" Ahmet shouted, completely mystified. The Contessa took advantage of his confusion by kicking the bazooka out of his gasp, sending it spinning across the floor.

"Behold the hide of the Nemean Lion!" cried Dr. Xenos. His

green eyes blazed through the tangle of golden fur covering his face. "In the first of his labors, Hercules fought this magnificent beast, which is covered by a pelt that is completely impervious to all weapons."

* * * *

"Stupid asshole vampires," Red Eye said as crept up the stairs leading to the roof of the club. He'd managed to sneak past the bloodsuckers and their enemies while they were fighting. Once he'd reached the roof, axe in hand, he made headed straight for the refrigeration control room. The room was dark, dank and filled with frost-coated pipes. In the middle of the room was a huge tank which held the liquid nitrogen that cooled the walls of the club.

Red Eye took his axe and began to hack at the floor with the axe. Soon, he'd created several holes in different parts of the room that would allow any escaping, dangerous fluids—like, say, deadly liquid nitrogen—to drain down through the building into the club below.

He then delivered several deep gashes to various pipes throughout the system. He ran out as the steaming, boiling, super-cool liquid began to gush forth and pour down into the club.

Red Eye then returned to the roof and headed straight to the helicopter. He climbed inside and looked for the ignition.

Happily, the idiots had forgotten to take the keys with them.

Back when he'd worked for hospital emergency rooms, his key duty was flying rescue helicopters.

He climbed in the driver's seat and flew off to begin his life anew.

CHAPTER EIGHTEEN

The Ninth Head of the Hydra

The Club Contessa
Las Vegas, Nevada

The golden hide of the Nemean Lion quickly melted away from the body of Dr. Xenos. The hair didn't fall to the floor—it simply returned to the dimension of myths and dreams.

Renfield rose from behind the bar. "I used to be a bartender," he said to vampire. "Can I fix you a drink?"

"What I want to drink doesn't come in a bottle," the red-haired man replied.

"Surely you'd enjoy like some fine, aged brandy," Ahmet said, flinging a crystal decanter at Dr. Xenos. The container smashed against his forehead, dousing the vampire with alcohol.

"You're really pissing me off," the vampire said, moving closer.

"All the more reason to chill out with some cocktails. How about some rum? Or vodka?" he said, throwing bottles and scoring two more hits. The vampire was quickly becoming a walking cocktail. "We also have some delightful liqueurs…"

"Ulfr and Shaitan!" the Contessa called to her wolves, who were sharing the throne as they watched the humans fight. "Attack! Attack!" she commanded, pointing to Ahmet. Her pets leaped from the marble stage and headed toward the chauffeur, who quickly pulled out his Ruger LCP Pistol and fired it twice. He hit one wolf in the head and the other in the heart. The beasts died side by side.

The Contessa ran over to the dead wolves. She cried tears as she cradled their heads in her arms. Soon her white dress was drenched with blood.

"You killed my babies! You will pay dearly for that!" She ran to her throne and raised her hand to push a red button on the armrest. This button opened multiple deadly trapdoors in the dance floor.

Before she could hit the button, a panel in the ceiling above her broke open, releasing a torrent of liquid nitrogen.

The Contessa screamed as the deadly frozen gas covered her body. Within seconds she was frozen solid. Her body then toppled over and broke into thousands of brittle red fragments.

"No!" screamed Dr. Xenos upon seeing the fate of his beloved. "My darling is dead! Dead! You fools shall pay for this! I will subject you to a thousand, a *million* torments! From this moment on, you will spent the rest of your pathetic lives screaming with endless pain! You will wish you had never been born!"

Renfield threw two more bottles of brandy at the vampire, saturating the monster with booze. Then he grabbed a black matchbox from the bar. The elegant little box was emblazoned with an elegant ice-blue *Club Contessa* logo.

"Talk, talk, talk," Renfield said. "You are one chatty bloodsucker.

But maybe *this* will shut you up."

So saying, he struck a match and tossed it at Dracula. The vampire was instantly enveloped in billowing flames.

Ahmet walked to his employer's side. "Dude, that was sweet. You totally cooked him!"

Renfield pointed toward the Contessa's shattered, scattered remains. "I don't really know what happened over there, but I'll assume that was all your doing."

Ahmet smiled. "Sure, I'll take the credit. Why not?"

Renfield pointed to the vampire, who was still standing and holding up the medallion. "Damn him, why won't he just *die?* What's he doing now?"

"My thanks!" the vampire cried to Renfield. "Your sins were so robust, I still have enough power in the medallion for one more transformation. Farewell for now. But I assure you: we shall meet again."

Wings of flame grew from the vampire's back. These were the wings of yet another powerful creature from Greek mythology: the Phoenix, a majestic, immortal bird capable of rising, newly born, from its own ashes.

Still clutching the medallion, Dracula flapped his mighty wings. Reborn yet again, he soared through one of the club's broken windows, out into the endless night.

AFTERWORD, BY C. DEAN ANDERSSON

Abbott And Costello Meet Dracula Transformed

Thinking back to when I was a kid, the film that first scared me enough to get my attention and attract me to horror was not any of the traditional horror classics. Well, it is classic now, but not then, just one in a series of Abbott and Costello films, the one where they meet Frankenstein (not the good Doctor, but the Monster as commonly misnamed, played by Glenn Strange, later the bartender in the Long Branch on TV's *Gunsmoke*, where the Marshal was played by the Vegetable Man from Mars in *The Thing*, James Arness).

In the same film, not only do A&C meet Frankenstein, our bumbling "Who's On First?" duo also meet Dracula, played by Bela Lugosi (only the second time he had played that famous role in a film, believe it or not), the Wolf Man, played by Lon Chaney, Jr., and at the end, for a brief moment, the Invisible Man, voiced by Vincent Price.

Abbot And Costello Meet Frankenstein, originally released in 1948, is a comedy film, but it was not funny the first time I saw it on an old black-and-white TV. You see, I had never seen these monsters before! So when, near the first, I saw Lawrence Talbot transform into the Wolf Man, I was not prepared to see a man become a hairy, befanged monster, and it scared me silly.

The scene is hilarious, now, as Talbot is on the telephone talking to Costello when the transformation happens, and Costello thinks someone's dog has taken over the phone, snarling and growling on the other end. But my being scared silly by Talbot's transformation felt strangely good, so I kept watching, peeking through my fingers from behind a pillow on the couch, and soon, on that unforgettable late-night monster show aired out of Wichita, Kansas, hosted by a ghoulish long-before-Elvira pair billed as "The Host and Rodney," I also met Dracula and the Frakenstein Monster.

If we had been capable of recording films for replay, or buying DVDs (or video tapes), I would have found a way to scrape enough of my meager allowance and "doin' the chores" money together to get that film. But as it was, years passed before I saw it again, by which time, thanks to that film, I was a veteran of many other horror films on late-night TV, a couple in actual theaters, and many devoutly studied monster magazines such as *World Famous Creatures*, *Castle of Frankenstein*, and of course, Forrest J. Ackerman's *Famous Monsters of Filmland*. To the older me, *A&C Meet Frankenstein* was no longer the least bit scary. But it was and remains what it was meant to be, funny.

One almost wishes Dracula had succeeded in transferring Costello's brain into the Frankenstein Monster. Maybe the Monster could then have become a top-hatted "man about town" and performed "Puttin' On the Ritz," years before Peter Boyle and Gene Wilder got it done. And that is another example of humor mixed with horror— Mel Brooks' *Young Frankenstein*! Stuffed lovingly full of horror riffs, boy, does that film make us laugh. And the tradition has never stopped. I recently saw a New Zealand gem from 2015 called *Deathgasm*, nonstop horror and humor and Heavy Metal music.

Assuming you have read the stories in this book before reading this afterword, you don't need me to guide you to humor mixed with horror in book form, because you just experienced many fine examples. Not that everything in this tome will make you laugh. Far from it. There are some seriously creepy scenes and shocks between these covers. In *Dracula Transformed*, Mark McLaughlin and Michael McCarty created an outstanding series of stories that can make you laugh and scream at the same time, unless you are new to the game, as I was when I first saw *A&C Meet Frankenstein*. Then, I guess, you probably just screamed.

It would be difficult for me to choose a favorite from all of these tales, and no one asked me to do that, anyway. Plus, depending on my mood, one might appeal to me more today than another did yesterday. But, that said, and as much as I love the humorous approach mixed with the horror, the one story that has the least humor in it is the one that got stuck in my mind and won't go away.

I was truly captivated and developed great affection for "Lucy

Transformed," so much so that I found myself wishing the authors had used it as an introductory chapter to a longer story, as they did in the last story herein, "Dracula Transformed," or even made it into a full-length novel. I wanted to know what happened next!

"Lucy Transformed" was an unusual approach to telling Bram Stoker's *Dracula* from a fresh perspective. One thing I regretted in Stoker's *Dracula*, though I still love it dearly and have read it several times over the years, was that, other than in the introductory chapters with Harker at the Castle, the Count himself rarely speaks. This was also a criticism sometimes leveled at the otherwise excellent Hammer Dracula films. The late Sir Christopher Lee's Count Dracula has little to say in most of them, and nothing at all in the second one, *Dracula Prince Of Darkness*.

By the time the historical series was running its course, with *Scars Of Dracula*, then the modernized incarnations, *Dracula A.D. '72* and *The Satanic Rites Of Dracula* (a.k.a. *Count Dracula And His Vampire Brides*), the Count had a few more lines, but never really enough, for me. At least in Jess Franco's non-Hammer *Count Dracula*, Lee was given better dialogue, partly because Lee used text from Stoker's novel for some of the Count's speeches. Perhaps and this connection came to me as I wrote this just now, Dracula's not getting to say enough in these films as in Stoker's novel is why, in my own novel, *I Am Dracula*, there was nothing but Dracula's words, because I wrote it as his first-person account of his life, death, and beyond, to explain (to my own satisfaction) how and why he became a Vampire.

But in "Lucy Transformed," McLaughlin and McCarty have the Count eloquently speak as never before, as a loving father writing to his daughter! If you have read *Dracula*, you know the other side of the story and why, tragically (in my opinion) there are no more letters after the last one. So, what happens next? I like to think I can guess, and it's a kind of mutated version of another favorite classic film of mine, *Dracula's Daughter*. But really, judging from the stories in *Dracula Transformed*, the authors would undoubtedly be more inventive than I can imagine, and in truth what happens next after "Lucy Transformed" ends is uncharted territory. So, maybe the authors will eventually continue the story (hint, hint). But if not, the ending is poignant and powerful enough to fire the imagination in unexpected ways on its own. "Leave 'em Wantin' More" is an old showbiz rule. Well, they did!

For all the humor and horror dished out *in Dracula Transformed,* one of the best things about the book as a whole and the stories on their own is that very special quality the best fiction always has: it makes you think, and it lets you see things you thought you knew differently forever afterward. Read these stories and then, the next time some ordinary thing crosses your path, some THING that starts out "normal" in one of these stories, only to become something horribly other, see if you don't find yourself looking at that ordinary thing in your "real world" in a new and different way. A general warning: in some cases, you may no longer feel comfortable turning your back on whatever "ordinary" thing is involved, but that's showbiz for you (heh, heh), thank goodness.

On the other hand, if you have not yet read the stories in *Dracula Transformed* but read this afterword first, because you sometimes cheat by starting from the back of a book and reading forward (which, I must confess, I sometimes do), you're now ready to treat yourself to the fine fare in this book (or read favorite stories herein again), because I'm almost done.

Yes, it is now time to re-greet or meet McLaughlin's and McCarty's collection of transformative tales of humor and horror. And by the way, it's okay to peek through your fingers a bit, if you have to. Courage! But however you wish to do it, and in whatever order, just go have some FUN!

ACKNOWLEDGMENTS

"Introduction" by The Amazing Kreskin and "Afterword: Abbott and Costello Meet Dracula Transformed" by C. Dean Andersson were written expressly for this collection.

The following stories have not been published before:

"Lucy Transformed" by Michael McCarty & Mark McLaughlin

"Incident in the Back of a Black Limousine" by Michael McCarty & Mark McLaughlin

"Dracula Transformed" by Mark McLaughlin & Michael McCarty

The following stories have been previously published:

"The Moon Is Our Mother" by Mark McLaughlin originally appeared in *Bizarre Bazaar* No. 1 (1992).

"Scrawny Goon in Dark Glasses" by Mark McLaughlin originally appeared as "Help Wanted" in *Plots* No. 1 (1990).

"Venus" by Mark McLaughlin originally appeared in the collection, *Slime After Slime* by Mark McLaughlin (Delirium Books, 2005).

"A Swim in the Moonlight" by Mark McLaughlin originally appeared in *Atopos* #1 (1991).

"In the Gutter" by Mark McLaughlin originally appeared in *Wicked Mystic* (1992_.

"Dracula, Inc." by Michael McCarty originally appeared in the collection, *A Hell of a Job* by Michael McCarty (Caliburn Press, 2010).

"Wanted: Undead or Alive" by Michael McCarty originally appeared in the collection, *Laughing In The Dark* by Michael McCarty (Damnation Books LLC, 2014).

"Dracula Has Risen from the Sofa" by Mark McLaughlin & Michael McCarty originally appeared in the collection, *A Little Help from My Fiends* by Michael McCarty (Wildside Press, 2014).

ABOUT THE AUTHORS

Mark McLaughlin's fiction, nonfiction, and poetry have appeared in more than 1,000 magazines, newspapers, websites, and anthologies, including *Cemetery Dance, Living Dead 2, Black Gate, Galaxy, Fangoria, Writer's Digest, Midnight Premiere, Dark Arts, In Laymon's Terms,* and two volumes each of *The Best Of HorrorFind* and *The Year's Best Horror Stories* (DAW Books).

Print collections of Mark's fiction include *Hideous Faces, Beautiful Skulls; Best Little Witch-House In Arkham; Beach Blanket Zombie; Motivational Shrieker; Slime After Slime; Pickman's Motel*; and *Raising Demons For Fun And Profit.* Also, Mark is the coauthor, with Rain Graves and David Niall Wilson, of *The Gossamer Eye,* which won the 2002 Bram Stoker Award for Superior Achievement in Poetry.

Mark has authored numerous Kindle story collections, including *The Abominations Of Nephren-Ka, The Horror In The Water Tower, Drunk On The Wine That Pours From My Wicked Eyes, Foreign Tongue,* and more.

With regular collaborator Michael McCarty, Mark has written *Monster Behind The Wheel, Attack Of The Two-Headed Poetry Monster, Revenge Of The Two-Headed Poetry Monster, All Things Dark & Hideous, Professor LaGungo's Classroom Of Horrors, Partners In Slime,* and more.

Mark has written numerous poetry collections, including *Phantasmapedia, Professor LaGungo's Exotic Artifacts & Assorted Mystic Collectibles,* and *Men Are From Hell, Women Are From The Galaxy Of Death.*

An accomplished artist, Mark has created artwork for the covers of many of his books. He is also a successful marketing and public relations executive who writes articles for business journals, newspapers, trade publications and websites.

You can befriend Mark at **www.facebook.com/markmclaughlinmedia.** Be sure to visit his Amazon.com Author's Page at **www.amazon.com/author/markmclaughlinmedia**. Also, you can read his blog at **www.BMovieMonster.com.**

* * * *

Michael McCarty has been a professional writer since 1983 and is the author of over thirty-five books of fiction and nonfiction, including *I Kissed A Ghoul; Laughing In The Dark; A Hell Of A Job; A Little Help From My Fiends; Dark Duets; Monster Behind The Wheel* (co-written with Mark McLaughlin); *Lost Girl Of The Lake* (co-written with Joe McKinney); *Conversations With Kreskin* (co-written with The Amazing Kreskin); The Scream Queen series: *Night of the Scream Queen* and *Return of the Scream Queen* (co-written with Linnea Quigley); The *Bloodless* vampire series: *Bloodless, Bloodlust* and *Bloodline* (co-written with Jody LaGreca); and *Liquid Diet & Midnight Snack: 2 Vampire Satires*. He is a five-time Bram Stoker Finalist and in 2008, he received the David R. Collins Literary Achievement Award from the Midwest Writing Center. He lives in Rock Island, Illinois, with his wife Cindy and pet rabbit Latte.

He is also the author of the mega-book of interviews, *Modern Mythmakers: 35 Interviews With Horror And Science Fiction Writers And Filmmakers*, which features interviews with Ray Bradbury, Dean Koontz, John Carpenter, Richard Matheson, John Saul, Bentley Little, Forry Ackerman, Adrienne Barbeau, Ingrid Pitt, C. Dean Andersson, Joe McKinney, Dan Curtis, Linnea Quigley, Christopher Moore, and more.

Michael McCarty is on Twitter as **michaelmccarty6**. His blog site is at **http://monstermikeyaauthor.wordpress.com**. On Facebook, you can Like him on his official page at **www.facebook.com/michaelmccarty.horror**. You can also snail-mail him at:

Michael McCarty
Fan Mail
P.O. Box 4441
Rock Island, IL 61204-4441

www.ingramcontent.com/pod-product-compliance
Lightning Source LLC
Chambersburg PA
CBHW020142180626
46810CB00004B/1693